Into the Beyond

Part I : Fated

Into the Beyond

Part I : Fated

Paul James Keyes

ISBN 978-1-952872-01-3

Published in the United States by Verge Publishing.
VergePublishing.org

Cover artwork by Paul James Keyes and Raven Wade Keyes.
Internal design by Paul James Keyes.

This is a work of fiction. Names, characters, places, and
incidents either are the product of the author's imagination or
are used fictitiously. Any resemblance to actual persons, living
or dead, events, or locales is entirely coincidental.

You can follow Paul on Twitter **@PaulJKeyes**,
TikTok **@PaulJamesKeyes**,
or visit **VergePublishing.org** to become an honorary
Chosen!

For my family,
thank you for helping me through the hard times.

Table of Contents

CHAPTER

1

Gray

Lines appeared in the air, each with a visibility waning less than the width of a spider's web. Faint as moonbeams, the lines were only observable if looked upon from just the correct angle. Any thinner and they would have ceased to exist in the visible realm altogether. But there they were, unlikely and peculiar, floating in the air like flecks of dust that inexplicably decided to cling together in a perfect row.

The light of dawn flooded in through the bedroom window and lit the improbable scene in a froth of gray that coalesced steadily as the maelstrom of lines unfolded. This was the time of morning when everything blended together—when the sun, though it was still below the horizon, threw its rays across the upper arches of the atmosphere, quickly turning the darkness of night into a new day. With every passing moment the sky brightened a little further and the bleak morning began to rouse even the darkest corners of the room.

Four of the ethereal lines met together, holding a fixed position in the center of the room. They joined at right angles, forming a square about two feet across. It shimmered ever so softly in the stale air. The other lines, each of varying length, began to spiral around this square base like wisps of smoke caught in a convection current. They moved like they were floating through water, but with an eerie intelligence, as if directed in motion by some unseen hand.

The square became more and more discernible as the remaining lines coiled around the ghostly structure. Once all the lines found their positions, the space between the four corners appeared to deaden. Light crossing the square's plane became dull and objects viewed through it were less defined as if covered by a filmy haze. This distortion was a property of the air; it rippled here, like waves of heat rising up from asphalt in the distance. Perhaps it was a trick of the light that caused these ripples; a mirage like the ones that brought hope to stranded desert travelers—dashing down one sand-dune and up the next in pursuit of some non-existent oasis.

On the opposite side of the room from where the semi-translucent square danced in silence, a narrow bed with blue sheets marked a very different enigma. The sheets, which appeared more black than blue in the faint morning light, were wrapped tightly around a young man, barely out of boyhood. Lewis Graham was still fast asleep despite the strangeness that was unfolding beside him. He did not look like a remarkable boy—in fact, he looked remarkably unremarkable—but eyes cannot always be relied upon to tell the full story when matters of destiny are involved.

As fate would have it, his life was about to change forever. Not more than six feet away from where he slept, a rift was beginning to open—a connection to the Beyond; to the realm of immortals.

Anyone observing would have seen an ordinary boy who woke up every day to the humdrum of a morning ritual—still half-asleep, he would brush his teeth with a frayed toothbrush and shower behind a mold-speckled shower curtain before drying off with a formerly red towel that had long since faded into a blotchy pink. He liked the color red, but it was no longer his favorite color as it had been when he was younger. He still couldn't make up his mind as to which color was his new favorite and so the point had become moot. After his shower he would quickly throw on whatever clothing smelled cleanest out of the pile accumulated in the corner of his bedroom, then run outside to catch the school bus to his high school—that is, assuming it was a weekday. He had done this once on a Saturday, and had since become considerably more careful about keeping track of the date.

He was not popular amongst his peers; not like his younger sister Jenny. Making friends did not come naturally to him like it did for her. Today was going to be the first day of a new school year—sophomore year of high school; a day which he had long been dreading ever since the first night of summer when he realized he would eventually have no choice but to return.

Even before the buzz of the first morning bell he would be thrown back in with the wolves—kids just gnashing their teeth to take a bite out of some easy prey like him. It was camaraderie through exclusion, dog-eat-dog mentality; kids seeking to beat down the weak to reestablish their superiority for the new year. Bullying was an everyday fact of life for Lewis. He was at the very bottom of the pecking order.

Lewis turned slightly in his sleep, pulling the covers up to his chin and shifted his legs so that his knees were bent halfway up to his chest. It was fortunate that he was still asleep, for what was about to unfold would have shaken even the most steadfast of men. Within the rippling air at the center of the square, a shape began to emerge. Nothing more than a blob at first; it was not yet clearly defined, just a dark outline. The space it occupied was un-solid; a flowing static field that flickered in and out of existence. The air throughout the room remained still despite the visual turbulence. There was no sound to indicate that anything unusual was happening.

The dark object sharpened further and further out of the static, as if getting closer. Tiny arms and legs appeared on a long torso. It was some sort of little creature. It remained perfectly still as its form became solid, the creature's face came into view; grotesque features appearing out of the darkness.

On its head were two beady eyes, spread wide and reflective like a cat's, but red in color. They contained no pupils. Below those were two holes which appeared to be nostrils on an otherwise nose-less face. It had a too-wide mouth with very thin lips, and at the top of its head was a tuft of stringy, black hair, all matted up into a tangled mess. The creature wore a little button-down suit which gave it the appearance of a large doll. The jacket was ragged around the edges with bits of frayed cloth sticking out randomly across its stitch lines. The creature's fingers were long and slender. It began to wiggle them ever so slightly as its form finished solidifying in the air.

With a deafening crack the outline of the square shot apart, vanishing in an instant. The creature fell to the ground as the rift closed.

Lewis sat up with a start.

The bedroom window shattered outward and books flew from the shelf. Lewis glanced around in confusion. Upon taking in the broken window, he cursed loudly. His mind had already drawn a logical conclusion as to the series of events that must have transpired. He stood up, pushed on his slippers, and ran over to the window. Scanning his eyes back and forth along the street below, he shouted angrily into the dawn air, "Who did that?" but there was no reply. Lewis walked back across the room, muttering more profanities under his breath before flipping on the light switch located just to the left of his bedroom door. Had he not been so sleepy, he may have noticed the lack of crunching glass beneath his slippers.

The creature was standing in the center of the room now, silently observing the boy. Lewis spotted it as soon as he turned around. "What the hell..." he said. At first he saw nothing more than a creepy doll. Its head was slightly larger in proportion to its body than a human's, and it had alabaster-white skin with a leathery appearance. Lewis approached the creature, unsure what to make of it. He assumed it must have been thrown through the window, though he had no idea how it miraculously landed so that it was standing up on its tiny feet. Lewis stooped his head down low to get a closer look. The creature, perfectly still up until this point, quickly craned its neck upward and looked Lewis right in the face. Lewis jumped backwards, banging his head hard on the dresser before falling to the ground and passing out from the shock.

He came to only moments later. The creature was now standing on his chest. "Lewis Graham," it said in a high-pitched, throaty voice. Lewis was gripped by fear in his chest, making him hold his breath. "Lewis Graham," it repeated, emotionlessly.

He threw the creature from him and began flailing his legs around in a panic as he scooted backwards towards the wall. The creature grunted as it skidded across the bedroom floor. Lewis was at a complete loss for words, "Who…? What…?" he gasped.

The creature stood up and dusted itself off, then took a couple of steps forwards. Lewis pressed his back up against the wall. "You are Lewis Graham," the creature rasped. It wasn't a question.

"How do you know my name?" asked Lewis.

The creature looked him up and down. "You are important, later," it muttered.

From down the hall outside of the bedroom came the annoyed voice of Lewis's father, Frank. "What's going on in there?" he asked.

"There's a…" Lewis didn't know what to say. "There's a *thing* in here… come quick!" he said, his voice full of panic.

The creature didn't move. It continued to stare at him from across the room. "No one else can see me," it said simply.

Lewis's father's hurried footsteps sounded down the hall as he rushed to his son's aid. The door swung open and he swept into the room with wide eyes, looking around wildly. His gaze drifted across the creature, unseeing, and didn't stop until it fell upon the shattered window with its glass broken outward. "Oh, Lewis! What did you do?"

"It wasn't me," he said. "That *thing* did it!" He pointed at the creature.

"I told you, he can't see me. Can't hear me either," it said. "You're making yourself look foolish."

Lewis's father wasn't amused. "Behaving badly isn't going to get you out of going to your first day of school," he said sternly. "And don't think you won't be paying for the window. It's coming directly out of your allowance." He looked over the damage once more, shaking his head. "I have to get up for work in…" he glanced at the clock on the wall, "thirty minutes." He sighed, as tired as he was irritated. "I'll deal with this later. Keep it down." He walked out of the room without giving Lewis another chance to say a word, shutting the door behind him as he went.

Lewis and the creature continued to stare at one another until after the house fell silent. "What are you?" Lewis finally asked in a hushed voice.

The creature smiled; it was an unnatural expression for its tiny face. "We have been called many things, and will be called many more before the end," it said, "Moirae, Parcae, Fates. My name is Longinus, but you may call me Mr. Gray." The creature smiled again. It… he… appeared to be making the unsettling expression in an attempt to put Lewis at ease rather than from an actual sense of amusement.

Lewis stared at the odd creature, and he stared right back at him, unblinking. "I must still be asleep," said Lewis. It was the only logical conclusion.

"You are not sleeping," said Mr. Gray, "although even in a waking state, humans do have quite a low level of awareness."

Lewis continued to stare blankly at the creature.

"Just like talking to a rock, aren't you?" he said, curling his lips up ever so slightly.

Lewis frowned. "What do you want?" he asked.

The creature smiled again, though this time he actually seemed to be amused. He opened his mouth slightly, displaying a set of jagged teeth that looked like splintered wooden pegs. His eyes flashed as he spoke. "It is not a question of what I want," he said, "but rather, what *you* want." Lewis was confused. Mr. Gray continued, "I am here to guide you. To make sure you fulfill your destiny."

"Destiny?" asked Lewis.

"Don't worry," said Mr. Gray. "There's no reason we can't have some fun in the meantime."

Lewis shook his head slightly, his vision becoming fuzzy as he tried to absorb what was happening. After a moment, he refocused back in on the creature. "What is my destiny?" he asked earnestly.

Mr. Gray waved his hand dismissively. "We'll get to that soon enough," he said. "I'm starving. How about you get me something to eat before it's time to start getting ready for school? It's going to be a good day!"

CHAPTER

2

Morning

I'm losing my mind, thought Lewis. There was no way Mr. Gray could be real. The two-foot-tall creature followed behind him spryly as he quietly opened his bedroom door and walked downstairs to the kitchen to retrieve the requested snack.

"Sugar cubes."

Definitely losing my mind. Mr. Gray had to be a figment of his imagination. The creatures brown shoes, laced tight to his tiny feet, made no sound as he walked. He seemed perfectly comfortable wandering through Lewis's house, uninvited as he was. He was too small to walk down the stairs with a normal stride. He hopped between steps, one at a time, landings softly on each of the carpeted surfaces until he was finally at the bottom. Lewis watched him curiously. *Funny little guy,* he thought. He probably would have been more concerned with the situation had he not been certain Mr. Gray was only in his head.

Once in the kitchen, Lewis pointed to the jar by the coffeemaker that held the sugar. Mr. Gray lifted his hands above his head like a toddler, requesting a lift up onto the counter. Lewis bent down apprehensively. He half-expected his hands to pass right through the creature when he tried to grab him, but he was, in fact, solid. He weighed less than the Graham family's large orange tabby cat, Melon. His patchwork jacket was soft to the touch. He placed Mr. Gray down next to the sugar jar and watched with amusement as his slender fingers quickly opened the container and began to rummage around inside. He retrieved a cube, looked it over carefully, and then placed it into his jacket pocket. It filled his pocket, leaving a large lump visible at his side. He then went back in to grab another one to munch on.

"Hey," came a whisper from behind him.

Lewis jumped. He spun around to find his sister, Jenny, at the base of the stairs, staring at him, sleepy-eyed.

"What was that noise?" she asked. Jenny was one year younger than Lewis, but she had never acted like a typical little sister. She was bossy.

Lewis's eyes shifted back to Mr. Gray, still munching away happily on his sugar cube. "She can't see or hear me either," he said between bites. "Only you can."

Lewis looked back at Jenny. He didn't know how to answer his sister's question. "A tiny creature blew out my window." He knew he sounded absurd.

Jenny stared back at him, unblinking. "You are so weird," she said. "I love you, but you should really try not to say stuff like that. Not around anyone anyway. No one's going to want to be friends with you if you're weird."

It was sad to Lewis that his little sister was giving him advice on making friends. She would be starting as a freshman. He should have been giving her the pep talk. She must have seen the downtrodden look that fell across his face.

"It'll be okay," she said as she walked over to him, "it's a new year. A new chance to make a good first impression. If you start being more social now, people will come around." She placed a consoling hand on his shoulder before glancing over at the open sugar jar. She picked up the lid, sitting on the counter beside Mr. Gray, and placed it back on top of the jar before grabbing a glass from out of the cupboard and filling it with water at the sink. "Just try to avoid Landon. If people see him picking on you, it might set the tone for everyone else for the whole year again." Jenny flashed him a sad smile before disappearing back upstairs to her room.

"Don't worry about Landon today," Mr. Gray added after Jenny was gone. "Once you do everything I say, you have a much better day than him." It was perplexing to hear Mr. Gray talk as if the day had already happened.

The flap of the cat door opening sounded from down the hallway. Mr. Gray's head turned sharply. His black, stringy hair flipped to one side of his head. Melon, probably thinking Lewis was his father, came trotting down the hall into the kitchen to his food bowl. The cat stopped short of his bowl, immediately taking notice of Mr. Gray, perched high on the counter. Mr. Gray stared back guardedly. Melon took a slow step forward, inching closer. Lewis could see the tension growing in Mr. Gray's body as Melon lowered his hindquarters to the floor, readying to pounce.

With a surprisingly graceful leap for the large cat, Melon hopped up onto the counter, directly on top of Mr. Gray before he could react. Mr. Gray screeched horribly as Melon flattened him to the counter. For a moment, Lewis was worried Melon intended to bite Mr. Gray, but his concerns dissolved immediately once Melon began tenderly licking the creature's alabaster face instead of sinking in his teeth.

"Get him off of me!" Mr. Gray cried out.

Lewis had to hold back his laughter. Apparently he wasn't the only one who could see Mr. Gray after all. The confirmation that Mr. Gray was real sent a shiver down his spine. He reached over and nudged Melon with the back of his hand until the cat stepped off Mr. Gray with a disgruntled meow.

"Horrible creature," Mr. Gray spat. "You leave me alone!" Mr. Gray hopped down from the counter unaided. He landed softly on his feet and then scampered quickly over to the stairs. Lewis followed behind him, leaving Melon alone in the kitchen. Mr. Gray struggled to climb several of the steps before Lewis scooped him up and carried him the rest of the way back to his room.

He stepped carefully over a squeaky patch in the floor in front of his parents' room. He didn't want to get in any more trouble by waking his father again. He moved as quietly as possibly to his open door and slipped inside.

"You were talking about my destiny?" Lewis prompted after placing Mr. Gray back down and closing his door.

Mr. Gray waved his hand dismissively. "Don't worry about that yet," he said. "I will keep you on track—just do everything I tell you."

Lewis nodded slowly, completely unsatisfied with the answer. "So you're a fate? Like the three fates of Greek mythology?"

"Yes, yes," said Mr. Gray, "they are my kind. We guide humans from time to time to keep everything running smoothly. Immortals visit your realm more frequently back then." Mr. Gray walked over to Lewis's backpack and unzipped it without giving any explanation. He removed a binder and pencil pouch and tossed them both aside with a tiny grunt.

"What are you doing?" asked Lewis.

Mr. Gray ignored the inquiry as he stepped into the backpack and sat down. "Wake me when you get to school," he said. He reached a hand out and zipped the bag most of the way shut before retracting his fingers back through the opening. The dismissal was final.

Lewis still wasn't certain that he wasn't going insane. His head ached where he bashed it on the dresser. Maybe Mr. Gray was just a night terror lingering around extra long because of the head trauma. It didn't really make sense, but Lewis didn't know what else to think.

There was an hour left before he needed to get up for school, so he turned out the light and got back in bed. He glanced over at his backpack. He could just make out one of the creature's red eyes peeking at him through an inch-wide opening.

Another shiver ran down his spine.

The eye withdrew as Mr. Gray settled down deeper into the bag. Lewis stared at his backpack for several minutes before turning over to face the wall. It was a bit disconcerting knowing he wasn't alone in his room. He didn't even let Melon in at night. His room was the only place where he got to withdraw from everyone and everything. His safe place had been invaded. As creepy looking as the strange creature was, he seemed harmless enough, at least.

Although Lewis had no expectation of being able to fall back asleep, short on rest, he soon felt his eyelids growing heavy, and before he knew it, he'd somehow managed to drift off again.

***

Lewis woke up, yawning as his mom, Betty, knocked on his door.

"Time to get ready for your first day of school!" she said enthusiastically from out in the hall.

Lewis rolled over. "I'm awake," he said groggily. His dreams had been so vivid.

A breeze blustered into the room and rustled his hair. His eyes shot across the room to the busted out window.

Mr. Gray... he can't have been real....

He hopped out of bed and ran over to his backpack. His hands were shaking slightly as he slowly shifted the zipper open and peered inside.

Empty.

A wave of relief washed over him. Only his school supplies were present.

It must have all been a crazy dream....

He couldn't explain the broken window, but with no Mr. Gray present, it *must* have all been in his head.

CHAPTER

3

An Extraordinarily Average Day

The morning went by as normally as any first day of school could. Lewis took a shower, ate a banana, and rode bus number fifty-two to his school, Edmonds-Woodway High. He waited in a long line in the cafeteria with the rest of the student population to pick up his class schedule and then made his way towards Mrs. Kerry's first period English class.

Lewis stepped outside, cutting through the courtyard on his way to class. The eclectic group of loners that hung out in the courtyard watched him as he walked by. No words were exchanged. Lewis was a loner too, but he didn't really fit in with the courtyard kids or any of the other cliques for that matter. Mostly thanks to Landon, Lewis was ostracized by his peers.

He took in a deep breath, filling his lungs with the frosty air in an attempt to quell the emotion that was beginning to build in his chest. It was a strangely crisp morning for September in the usually temperate city of Edmonds. As much as Lewis had been dreading the start of school, he'd also been going a bit stir crazy at home alone all summer. Dry weather meant forest fires in Canada and northern Washington and an annoyingly smoky August throughout the Puget Sound. Indoor activities like reading and playing video games were the only options left for someone like Lewis who didn't have any friends.

Despite the trend of smoky summers—courtesy of climate change—Lewis felt fortunate to have grown up in Washington State. Nestled in the Pacific Northwest, Edmonds was full of all the small-town charm one could stomach, with beautiful views of the Olympic Mountains rising up across the shimmering blue waters of the Puget Sound. There was no beating an Edmonds sunset. The whole sky would light up pink and orange over the mountains and reflect off the water below—barring smoke of course. The ferry system made Edmonds a hub for many Seattle commuters. Sadly, big-city problems like crime and homelessness had slowly started to encroach in from the larger Seattle area over the past few years. When Lewis was younger, he wouldn't have thought twice about walking around late at night, but things had changed just enough to make the darkness feel malevolent.

Lewis kept to himself these days. He pretty much lived in his bedroom, only venturing out when he needed to. The conflicting drives of loneliness and social anxiety made for a bumpy morning.

In English class, Mrs. Kerry assigned Oedipus Rex for in-class reading. The Ancient Greek tragedy's themes of prophecy and fate immediately reminded Lewis of his crazy *dream* of Mr. Gray. The thought was fleeting, though, and

Lewis soon forgot all about the odd creature. He counted the number of students set to read ahead of him so that he could figure out which passage he would have to read in front of the class. He practiced it a few times in his head so that he wouldn't stumble over his words and embarrass himself. Embarrassment felt worse than death to Lewis—such was high school life. English soon ended and he continued on with his ordinary day.

Social studies with Mr. Garfield came next. Lewis spotted Landon Mathews sitting off to the side with some of the other jocks. He quietly made his way to the back of the room in an attempt to avoid his notice. Many years ago, before puberty and excessive weight lifting chiseled Landon's body into the annoyingly handsome, Greek hero-like physique he now possessed, Landon and Lewis had been best friends. They sat next to each other on the bus on the first day of kindergarten and were soon inseparable. They remained best friends until the third grade when Landon suddenly realized that bullying Lewis made him more popular with the rest of the kids. He used everything he knew about Lewis to ridicule him in front of his peers and never once got in trouble for his tormenting. Lewis learned long ago that the world wasn't a fair place.

"Sup, Lewser," said Landon from across the classroom. A chorus of snickers arose from the other students. The teacher, Mr. Garfield, was ancient, half-deaf, and completely useless to Lewis. Landon pushed his medium length pretty-boy hair off his forehead as he smirked at Lewis. "Did you get your tighty-whities out of your crack yet, or are you still flossing with them?" Full-on laughter erupted in the classroom. Mr. Garfield looked around confused.

Lewis didn't even wear full briefs, but Landon had given him a wedgie so hard over the summer when he spotted him at the grocery store that the band of his boxer briefs partially tore. There was nothing that Lewis could say without making things worse.

"Settle down," ordered Mr. Garfield. "We are going to play an ice-breaker game and then go over the syllabus for the semester." He had everyone count off to form groups. Landon and Lewis both ended up as fours and were placed in the back corner of the room. "These will also be your groups for your semester-long project, worth forty percent of your grade."

Lewis sighed. Landon didn't look any happier at least. He flicked Lewis painfully on the earlobe before sitting down beside him. "You're gunna do my part of the project," said Landon, "or else I'll make this year hell for you."

"Aren't you going to do that regardless?" Lewis asked sassily.

Landon flicked his ear again in response. Things were lining up to be the worst year yet for Lewis.

Lunch was next, and although Lewis didn't have any friends to sit with, he did have a routine he liked to follow. He made his way quickly to the cafeteria, but instead of stopping there he continued on down to the end of the hall to a bank of vending machines. He waited off to the side, trying to look as inconspicuous as possible while he waited for one particular student to arrive.

McKenzie Spencer, better known as Kenzie, was a blonde firecracker, recent addition to the cheer squad, and all around heartthrob as far as Lewis was concerned. He'd had a crush on her for years, but hadn't built up the courage to do anything about it yet. This year was going to be the year. She'd just broken up with Jeff Doyle over the summer and it was the first time since Lewis first saw her in middle school that she'd actually been single. Lewis had been coming to this vending machine every lunch since halfway through freshman year when he realized Kenzie frequented the location to pick up a sports drink.

Lewis had never had a class with Kenzie, but his heart skipped beats whenever he was around her. He had a plan to make a good impression. As soon as he spotted her coming down the hall he pulled four dollars out of his wallet and quickly fed two of them into the machine. He pushed the button for the blue colored one—Kenzie's go-to flavor. He didn't pick it up after it fell to the bottom of the machine—instead he started feeding in the next two dollars. Kenzie stepped up behind him. He could feel her presence, but didn't turn around yet as the machine accepted his money and he pressed the blue option yet again. His heart was beating out of his chest as the drink fell and he reached into the compartment at the bottom.

"Oh, crazy," he said, saying the script that had been repeating in his head all summer, "a second one fell." He grabbed both bottles and began to turn around. "Would you like—?" He suddenly realized that it was not Kenzie standing behind him… it was Landon.

"Don't mind if I do, dingus," said Landon. He snatched both bottles out of Lewis's hands before trotting over to Kenzie, who'd been sidetracked talking to her friends down the hall.

"Here you go, babe," said Landon, handing one of the bottles to Kenzie before kissing her gratuitously on the lips.

Lewis felt as if he was sinking into the floor. Everything was ruined. He wanted to cry with frustration. He moved quickly back past the cafeteria, trying to get as far away from Landon and Kenzie as he could before stopping. He went outside to the courtyard and climbed the stairs by the main office before sitting down and considering what this all meant. Landon and Kenzie were dating. The girl of his dreams was with the boy of his nightmares. He wanted to go home and lock himself in his room, if only that were an option.

He opened his backpack, part of him half-expecting to see Mr. Gray as he retrieved his lunch. He shook his head at his own silliness. *Even if Kenzie was still single and not dating my mortal enemy, what chance do I really have? I'm the weird kid with no social skills or friends. She wouldn't want to date me, or even talk to me!*

He wasn't feeling hungry, but only had twenty minutes left before his last class of the day, Chemistry, so he forced himself to eat the turkey sandwich his mother packed him. He choked it down. It was dry without having anything to drink with it. When he was finished, he shoved the empty paper bag back in his backpack and made his way into the building across from the office that housed the theater and woodshop classrooms. There was a water fountain in there where he could quench his thirst.

While drinking, he heard the door open behind him. Several other students walked in silently. He didn't think anything of it until someone grabbed the back of his head and slammed his face down into the water fountain's metal basin. His chin took the brunt of the hit. He gasped as cold water covered his face and shot up his nose. The hand released him and he spun around.

Landon and two of his jock cronies had him trapped. There was a strange look in Landon's eyes. "Stay away from my girl, Lewis," he said. "I saw what you were trying to do earlier. If I so much as see you looking at her again, there's gunna be hell to pay."

Landon glanced around to make sure no teachers were watching and then gestured to his cronies with his head. They each grabbed ahold of one of Lewis's arms and dragged him to the empty woodshop classroom, then threw him down on the floor. Landon began messing with the door. By the time Lewis was back on his feet, the three bullies were laughing and giving each other high-fives.

"Sleep tight," said Landon.

They slammed the door shut on Lewis. The laughter continued as he heard them walking back down the hallway and out of the building. Lewis immediately tried the door, but of course, it was now locked. Next, he tried his cellphone, which he found inexplicably dead. He didn't know what to do. Woodshop wasn't taught in the afternoons. There was a chance nobody would come by until the following morning unless a janitor was scheduled to clean the building. Being that this was the first day of school, Lewis doubted his chances.

Lewis spent the remainder of lunch period searching for a way out. None of the windows opened and without a key, the door was impassable.

Soon, the bell for last period rang. Defeated, Lewis sat down on a stool—there weren't even any normal chairs in the classroom. Tears began to flow down his cheeks. He had known Landon was going to make the day terrible, but he never could have imagined that he would go this far. He couldn't fathom what could drive a person to be so cruel.

Crack!

The sound was deafening. Lewis fell from his stool as the shock startled him.

"Hello, Lewis Graham," said the high-pitched voice of Mr. Gray.

Lewis was even more surprised than he'd been that morning. He'd put the whole encounter behind him, explaining it away as just an odd dream.

"I apologize for disappearing on you," Mr. Gray said. "I was attending to details."

Lewis found himself speechless again. He couldn't believe what he was seeing. The tiny creature walked over to a cabinet at the side of the room and immediately pulled out the key to the woodshop classroom door.

"Let's get started," said Mr. Gray. "Such fun we have today." The creature giggled mischievously.

Lewis shrugged. "Alright," he said. *Today can't get any worse, I guess.* "Lead the way."

CHAPTER

4

A Vague Warning

Lewis decided that regardless of whether he was hallucinating or dreaming he was going to make the most of his time with the seemingly omnipotent creature. Mr. Gray cautioned against walking past the main office, so Lewis took the steps back down into the courtyard instead. The halls were empty of students with final period having already started.

Mr. Gray was back inside Lewis's backpack, his head poking out this time, so that he could give him instructions while he walked. "Wait by the door and don't go back inside until exactly twelve thirty-four," he said. "The day is better when you avoid the hall monitor."

Lewis checked his watch. He had two minutes to kill. "What about after that?" he asked. "I'm going to be in trouble for being late to chemistry."

Mr. Gray chuckled. "When you walk in, tell your teacher there was a mistake with your printed schedule and that you've corrected it. I nudged everything else into alignment already so you can enjoy the rest of the ride. I'll tell you when you need to say something specific."

Lewis did exactly as he was told. He waited until his watch read twelve thirty-four and then reentered the building. As he passed the restroom nearest his chemistry class he heard pained moans coming from inside the men's room.

Mr. Gray giggled again. "Just one of the details," he explained.

Lewis grimaced.

Despite Mr. Gray's assurance that everything would work out for the best, Lewis felt anxious as he approached the classroom door. He could hear Mr. Jenkins leading the class inside. He paused at the door and took a breath before entering. All eyes shifted to Lewis as he stepped inside. Mr. Jenkins was visibly annoyed by the interruption, his eyebrows lowering into a deep frown at the sight of him, but Lewis followed the script laid out to him by Mr. Gray. He spotted Landon on the far side of the room while he was speaking. *Another damn class with Landon?!* Luck did not seem to be on his side… but then again, Mr. Gray was here now. His tormenter had a sour look on his face.

Mr. Jenkins glanced around the classroom. Everyone was already split up into pairs, working on their first lab. "Is Jake still not back from the restroom?" he asked the class. Several kids shrugged or shook their heads. "I'm going to have to send someone out to track him down if he doesn't return soon," he mused. He looked back over at Lewis. "How about you take Jake's spot and partner with McKenzie, and I'll just give Jake extra homework if he comes back."

Lewis's eyes shot over to Jake's empty seat and found Kenzie staring back at him, doe eyed. Next he looked over at Landon. The bully's glare intensified as Lewis took Jake's seat.

"Let me out," requested Mr. Gray.

Lewis placed his backpack on the lab table and unzipped it. Mr. Gray hopped out spryly and stretched his arms.

"Enjoy yourself," suggested Mr. Gray before running off down the long lab table, leaving Lewis alone to chat with Kenzie.

Lewis kept his eyes on Mr. Gray. He watched curiously as the creature began to fiddle with the Bunsen burner over at Landon's station. Landon noticed Lewis peering his way and shot him another dirty look.

"How was your summer?" asked Kenzie, drawing his attention back.

Lewis swallowed the lump in his throat. "It was good," he said. "Low key. What about you?"

"Spent time at cheer camp, mostly. It was fun, but I missed the boys," she said with a smile.

Lewis blushed.

They started into their lab work. Being late, Lewis missed the first portion of the lab, but he was able to jump right into the second experiment, heating up a mixture of chemicals over their Bunsen burner. His fingers accidentally grazed up against Kenzie's as they both reached for the burner at the same time. Kenzie's hand was there first. They shared an awkward smile as Lewis retracted his hand, letting Kenzie take the lead with setting up the equipment.

Mr. Gray came trotting back over. "Ask for her phone number. Say it's so you can help each other out with the homework later."

Lewis blushed again just thinking about it, but he said the words.

"Sure," said Kenzie. She grabbed Lewis's arm and wrote her number on the palm of his hand, adding a little heart at the end.

Lewis wanted to jump with glee. Landon was not going to be happy. Lewis glanced over towards Landon's station once again just in time to see Landon's Bunsen burner flare up in a massive fireball. Mr. Gray danced back and forth in front of Lewis, squealing in delight. Landon's sleeve was engulfed with flames. Several students screamed as he rushed to the eyewash station and doused his entire arm with the spray-nozzle faucet. Although the fire was out, Landon still wore a pained grimace.

"Nurse's office, now," ordered Mr. Jenkins.

Lewis was shaken. He felt somewhat responsible for Mr. Gray's tampering. Still, he couldn't help but be amused by Landon catching on fire—if anyone deserved such a thing, it was Landon—but he wouldn't wish for anyone to be seriously injured.

Kenzie didn't look overly concerned that Landon had just been in flames. She merely rolled her eyes, ignoring the whole scene. "He's always doing something stupid," she said. Lewis had to wonder just how close they were.

While everyone else was watching Landon's misfortune, Lewis realized a girl in the back of the classroom was staring in his own direction instead. He'd never seen the girl before.

She was Native American—long, straight, dark hair hanging well below her shoulders. Her brow was furrowed with concern, but it did not appear to be for Landon. She turned away as soon as she noticed Lewis looking back at her, hiding her face in her textbook.

Lewis shook it off. He was used to negative attention.

The rest of class went by swimmingly, with Lewis sharing laughs with Kenzie. Mr. Gray told him snippets of things to say from time to time, just enough to keep the conversation rolling. Lewis had never felt so suave.

Before he knew it, class was over. Lewis was a little disappointed. He'd never spent so much time with Kenzie before, and he was feeling extra confident having Mr. Gray's guidance. He didn't want it to end! While Mr. Gray was busy packing himself away in Lewis's backpack, the Native girl he'd caught staring at him earlier brushed past him and slipped a folded piece of notebook paper into his hand. Lewis cocked his head in confusion. When he looked up, the girl was glancing back his way. Her wide-eyed expression was wrought with worry. Lewis realized in an instant that she was not looking at him, but directly at Mr. Gray, sitting snug in his pack. In another instant she had rushed out the door and disappeared into the throng of students already in the hallway outside.

Lewis hefted his backpack up, securing Mr. Gray to his back before nonchalantly unfolding the note:

Don't trust it.

The vague warning sent a shiver down his spine. By the time he exited the classroom, the girl was nowhere to be found.

CHAPTER

5

Consequences

The note made Lewis much less confident in his decision to listen to Mr. Gray. The odd creature had already scored him considerable face-to-face time with Kenzie, and lit Landon on fire—not to mention saving him from the woodshop. All positive things, although the fire was a little scary. The way Mr. Gray danced with such joy as Landon burned was downright creepy. There was no love lost between Lewis and Landon, but Lewis still didn't want to see the bully maimed— he simply wasn't that cruel.

The girl's warning did not fall on deaf ears, but Lewis wasn't ready to completely abandon Mr. Gray's advice. What should have been one of the worst days of his life had turned into one of the best he could remember in the blink of an eye.

Kenzie knows who I am! And she gave me her number! With a heart!

Lewis began walking towards the school bus loading area. After just a few steps, he heard Mr. Gray's distinctive high-pitched voice in his ear. "Go to the student parking lot instead."

The direction seemed harmless enough. He changed course, walking past the cafeteria and down the hall to the exit nearest the student parking lot. Once outside, Mr. Gray directed Lewis to take him out of his backpack and place the pack open on the ground beside him on the curb. Lewis had no idea where this was going, but he obliged.

"What next?" asked Lewis.

"Just stand here," said Mr. Gray. "Face the driving lane and wait."

Lewis's mind was filled with questions. *Is someone going to offer me a ride? Will it be Kenzie? Does she even have her driver's license yet?*

Lewis flinched as his backpack flew into the street—kicked. His school supplies skittered all across the lane.

Landon's annoying chuckle rang out. "Watch where you leave your junk," he said.

Lewis turned around. Landon and his cronies were behind him. Kenzie was just stepping out of the school behind them as well. Mr. Gray hadn't given him any other instructions.

"Landon Mathews!" shouted Coach Phillips. He was the football coach, but often worked as the parking lot attendant as well when he wasn't teaching Physical Education. "What do you think you're doing, young man? You better apologize to that boy and pick up his stuff!"

Landon's face went white. He was on the football team and knew better than to disobey Coach Phillips. Landon's cronies snickered to themselves at Landon's expense as he said a disingenuous "sorry" and walked over to retrieve Lewis's belongings. Coach Phillips watched with crossed arms. A small crowd was forming along the curb. Landon worked quickly. He grabbed the last of Lewis's pens and tossed it into the bag with everything else. As he stood up, the rumble of an accelerating engine was the only warning he received before a small truck careened directly into him.

Landon's arm and head rebounded violently off the hood of the vehicle. His shoes flew off as he was launched forward into the air. Everyone gasped as the truck took a sharp left, and sped off down the length of the student parking lot and out into the main street.

All Lewis saw was a flash of blue inside the truck's cabin. The driver had a blue hoodie drawn up over his or her head.

"Good work," said Mr. Gray.

Lewis was mortified.

Coach Phillips and several students ran over to Landon. He was lying in a twisted heap. The pavement was already painted red with blood from his head.

"Stay back!" shouted Coach Phillips as he reached Landon's side.

Lewis hadn't moved. To him, the whole world had fallen silent. He was too horrified to even breathe. The crack of Landon's head as it struck the metal truck was enough to make him nauseous.

A girl standing next to him was already on her phone with the police. The hospital was literally across the street from the high school. Soon, the siren of an ambulance sounded and a mere thirty seconds from that, paramedics were already on the scene. It all happened so fast, Lewis barely had time to take any of it in.

He overheard one of the paramedics say that Landon was still breathing as he was loaded, unconscious, onto a gurney and placed in the back of the aid car.

Mr. Gray is dangerous.

The creature stretched his legs one at a time and then cleared his throat to get Lewis's attention. "You did well so far today," he said once Lewis looked back over at him. "I'm going to leave you for a little bit, but I'll be back later tonight. There is still much fun to be had."

Lewis didn't like the sound of that. He was starting to understand Mr. Gray's idea of fun, and it didn't end well for the people around him. He wished the creature would just leave him alone. Although Lewis hadn't exactly been happy before meeting Mr. Gray, now he was more terrified than anything else.

His backpack was sitting on the ground two feet away from him. By the time he snatched it up, Mr. Gray had already vanished back into thin air. Lewis didn't know what to do. If Mr. Gray was as powerful as he seemed, Lewis was afraid of what might happen if he disobeyed one of the creature's commands.

CHAPTER

6

Seeking Answers

There were just eight kids on Lewis's bus. Only freshman and sophomores under the age of sixteen who didn't have their driver's licenses yet took buses home. Most of those took the city metro buses. Students who lived in areas that the metro buses didn't cover were the only ones who had to take the yellow school buses. If there were any fewer kids in Lewis's area, they probably would have had a van picking them up and dropping them off.

Lewis sat at the back of the bus across the aisle from his sister. No one else was aware of Landon's *accident* around the corner of the school.

"What happened to you?" asked Jenny. "You look weird."

Lewis shook his head. "Nothing. I'm fine." There wasn't anything he could say about his current predicament that wouldn't make him sound insane. They rode in silence for several minutes before Lewis got the bright idea to see if his sister knew anything about the Native American girl who'd snuck him the warning note.

Despite being unpopular, Lewis knew everyone in the sophomore class by sight if not by name. He didn't recognize the girl at all, so unless she was new, she must have been his sister's year and simply in advanced science placement.

"Hey, Jen?" he asked. She glanced over at him. "Is there a Native girl your year that might be in my chem class?"

Jenny raised an eyebrow. "There's only one that I know of that's my year. She was in advanced math in middle school, so I guess she's pretty smart. She could be in chem, I suppose. Why do you ask?"

"No reason, just curious," said Lewis.

Jenny continued to watch him incredulously. She was going to make him fish for more information, he just knew it. After another minute of silence he finally caved.

"Do you know her name?" he asked.

"Mhm," said Jenny. She didn't offer it to him.

"Are you going to tell me what it is?"

Jenny rolled her eyes. "I can see the phone number on your palm, duffus. You expect me to believe you got her number but not her name?"

Lewis closed his hand, hiding Kenzie's phone number. "That's not hers," he said. "I was just curious, geez." Jenny could be exasperating.

She was grinning now. "I'm impressed," she said. "You really made the most out of today, didn't you!?"

Lewis grimaced. *More than you know.*

"Fine, I'll tell you," she said. "Her name is Josie Mays. You should know, though, she has a bit of a reputation…. You'd be better off with whatever girl drew that tiny, teensy-weensy, cutie-pie heart on your palm."

Lewis buried his hand deep in his pocket.

"It's cute seeing you with a crush," said Jenny. "So… tell me more about Heart-Girl. Who is she?"

Lewis narrowed his eyes. "First, tell me more about Josie," he said.

Jenny shook her head dismissively. "You should seriously forget about Josie. Everyone knows she's weird. Most people my year avoid her. There's a rumor she killed her parents or something and that's why she lives with her grandfather now."

It was Lewis's turn to look incredulous.

Jenny elaborated. "I mean not like she slashed their throats or anything, but like they died in a car crash when she was little and it was her fault somehow. Only Josie lived."

Lewis balked at the insinuation. "So a little girl tragically loses her parents in a car accident and your entire class decides that makes her *weird* and ostracizes her for the rest of her life?"

"I mean…" Jenny stumbled over her words. "It's not like that. She just…. She acts weird and stuff. I don't know. I just know no one really hangs out with her because she's really odd."

"Mhm," said Lewis. "The same way I'm 'so weird'?"

Jenny gawked at him. "Don't bite my head off. I was just trying to do you a favor. If you don't start raising your status, high school's going to suck for you. Associating with Josie

Mays can only make things worse…. I'm not trying to be mean—it's just the way things are."

Lewis wasn't impressed with his sister's mentality. Sometimes he wondered if his lack of social skills was actually just a symptom of his disdain for putting up with immature, fake people. He never enjoyed the types of drama-filled games his peers were always playing with one another. It was much easier to bury himself in a good book or movie than it was to attempt to navigate the adolescent hell of high school gossip. Most kids his age were insufferable.

"Would you happen to know where Josie lives?" he asked.

Jenny frowned. "Who's Heart-Girl?" she asked stubbornly.

Lewis sighed. He knew she wasn't going to let it go. "Kenzie Spencer."

Jenny's eyes grew to the size of saucers. "Wow," she said, "I wasn't expecting that. Are you sure it's really hers?"

Lewis answered with a blank stare.

"I'm kidding," she said. "Nice going. Aiming high. Hope you don't fly too close to the sun."

"Thanks for the vote of confidence."

Jenny merely laughed.

"So… Josie's address?" he reiterated. Jenny began studying his face, clearly confused as to why he was so curious about Josie when he had a shot at possibly being with Kenzie. He felt like he was being dissected under a microscope, the way she looked at him. He quickly made up a lie. "She accidentally left her chemistry book behind in class and I need to give it back to her so she can do her homework," he said.

He hoped the excuse for his inquiry would make Jenny stop being so irritatingly difficult.

She continued studying Lewis's face for a moment longer but ultimately gave in. "She lives really close to us actually—just down past the creepy house a couple blocks. We're gunna drive right by it. I'll point it out."

Jenny never made things easy.

"Kenzie Spencer…" she mused, a permanent smirk etched into her face.

Jenny did as she promised, pointing out Josie's house as the bus drove past. Lewis did his best to memorize the location. He needed answers, and Josie was the only person he knew of who might have some. After getting off the bus in front of his house he ditched Jenny to go pay Josie a visit.

He walked quickly down his street, passing the creepy house without paying it much thought. The house, lovingly dubbed the *creepy house*, was a dilapidated structure, abandoned for many years. Its paint was peeling and faded from the weather. Tall grass covered the whole property. The mailbox was gone, or buried in the brush, and many of the house's windows were broken out and boarded shut. Kids sometimes dared one another to break into it because of an urban legend that a serial killer once lived there. It was said that his ghost still haunted the grounds. Lewis didn't believe any of that nonsense, but he still got a little creeped out if he ever walked past it on the near side of the street.

After passing the creepy house, it only took a few short minutes before he was on Josie's street. Her house was on the right. Its distinctive red bricks, unusual for the area, made it impossible to miss. While approaching the house, he could see Josie through a second story window. She was talking to someone and didn't appear to notice Lewis as he stepped up onto the front porch. He rapped his knuckles against the wooden door. An older man, presumably Josie's grandfather, answered the door with a frown on his face.

"Good afternoon, Mr. Mays," said Lewis, "I was wondering if I could speak to Josie."

Josie's grandfather looked Lewis up and down without saying a word.

"We're in chemistry together…" Lewis added.

"Josie's not home," said Mr. Mays. He shut the door in Lewis's face with an abrupt slam that made him stumble back in surprise. There wasn't a chance to mount any kind of protest.

Lewis was certain he'd seen Josie in the window upstairs.

Weird, thought Lewis, *maybe Jenny is right about this family.*

He wasn't used to adults being so impolite to him. It was more than a little unnerving. He felt his hands begin to shake as a sudden spike of adrenaline coursed through his veins—his body's too-late response to the shock of the rude dismissal.

He clenched his fists as he walked back out to the street. He shot one last glance up at Josie's window. He couldn't see her anymore and the light was off now. Given the fearful look on her face when she saw Mr. Gray earlier in class, Lewis supposed he couldn't really blame her for wanting to avoid him.

The lack of answers was disheartening as he headed back home. He gave the brick house one last curious glance from down the street.

What do you know, Josie Mays?

He didn't have any more time to ponder his predicament or the nature of Mr. Gray, as the creature was waiting for him on his bed when he arrived back at home.

"Right on time," said Mr. Gray. "Tonight is such fun," he squealed.

A nervous knot formed in Lewis's belly. After what happened to Landon, Mr. Gray's idea of fun was the last thing Lewis wanted to experience again.

CHAPTER

7

Primitive Science

Mr. Gray handed Lewis his phone charger. "Get it started up. You call Kenzie in exactly three minutes."

Lewis plugged his dead cellphone in. The boot-up logo appeared immediately. He glanced over at his window; still broken. His mother had taped a sheet of plastic over the opening with blue electrical tape while he was at school. Once his phone was fully on he opened up the dialing window and looked down to retrieve Kenzie's number from the palm of his hand. To his dismay, a large smudge ran across several of the digits, rendering them illegible. He wasn't usually one for clammy hands, but all the stress of having Mr. Gray around was doing weird things to him.

Mr. Gray grunted in what Lewis assumed was annoyance. His little feet sank into the blue comforter as he bounced over to Lewis. He snatched the phone out of his hand and tapped on the contacts app. Lewis was surprise to see Kenzie's number already added to his list. It was perplexing, seeing as how the phone had been dead in his pocket all day long. He glanced over at Mr. Gray, but wasn't able to read the creature's expression.

Lewis decided now was the time to mention his concerns. "Landon got hurt really bad today…." he said.

Mr. Gray stared at him, unblinking. "He deserved it." He tapped the phone and initiated a call to Kenzie before handing it back to Lewis. "Be natural," he said. "And for your sake, agree with everything she says. Everything."

Lewis liked it better when Mr. Gray was giving him more specific instructions on what to say. He was no good at talking to girls on his own.   His stomach filled with a tornado of disorderly butterflies as the phone rang several times.   Part of him hoped she wouldn't pick up, but with the call being Mr. Gray's doing, he knew that wouldn't be the case.

"Hello…?" Kenzie answered the call.

"Hey, Kenzie," he said. "It's Lewis… Lewis Graham… from class… chemistry…." He grimaced at his own awkwardness. "Your lab partner."

"Jake?" asked Kenzie.

"…your other lab partner. Lewis. You wrote your number on my hand…."

"Oh, hi, Lewis," she said. "I wasn't expecting you to call. Everyone usually texts…."

Mr. Gray interrupted, "Say you wanted to make sure she was doing alright after seeing what happened to Landon." It was eerie hearing the creature talk about the horrible incident so nonchalantly, as if he hadn't set the whole thing in motion.

Lewis repeated the words anyway.

"Oh, that's sweet," said Kenzie. "Yeah, I'm fine. I can't believe that happened though! Did you hear the police found the truck abandoned down the street? It was Mrs. Davidson's! Someone stole it—they're still looking for the driver, but no one got a good look."

Lewis shot Mr. Gray a glance. "No, I didn't hear that. That's crazy. Mrs. Davidson's the librarian, right?"

"Mhm," said Kenzie. "I wonder if she was the one driving. Maybe she's just pretending it was stolen. Librarians hate kids, right?"

That was about the stupidest thing Lewis had ever heard, but he followed Mr. Gray's instructions and agreed with her. "Yeah, maybe." He didn't know what to say next. It wasn't exactly his idea to make the call.

"Hey, I was wondering, do you like to drink?" Kenzie asked.

Mr. Gray prompted Lewis with a head nod.

"Yeah," Lewis lied, "sometimes."

"Ok, cool, I wasn't sure if you liked to party since you're new here. You moved here from California or something, right? I think someone told me that...."

Mr. Gray was nodding even more vigorously now.

"Uh huh," said Lewis, though it pained him greatly. Kenzie actually thought he was new to the school, despite having walked the same halls with him every day since middle school. It was humiliating and depressing that he'd made so little of an impression on her that she didn't even realize he existed until Mr. Gray began guiding him.

"So…" said Kenzie, her tone changing to a flirty giggle, "I'm having a small gathering tonight. Just a few friends. You can totally come by if you're interested."

Lewis didn't need Mr. Gray's prompting this time. "Yeah!" he exclaimed. "I'd love to!"

"Ok, great!" said Kenzie. "Oh hey, I gotta go and start setting things up. I'll see you later though."

"Oh, ok," said Lewis.

"I'll text you the time and address," she said before hanging up unceremoniously.

Lewis wasn't sure how to feel about what just happened. He wasn't sure if Kenzie thought he was someone else or if she was just confused for some other reason. Regardless, she did invite him over. He decided to chalk it up as a win.

A new text beeped in. Lewis checked the message: "c u@7" it read, followed by her address. He glanced through the conversation history. There shouldn't have been any other messages present, but strangely the phone had already received the very same message many times before. He started scrolling up through the texts, but it just repeated over and over again.

Some sort of weird glitch?

Things didn't quite add up.

"You must do your homework now. There isn't time later," said Mr. Gray.

Lewis put his phone away, despite the weird feeling in his gut. He opened his backpack to dig out his homework assignments. All of his teachers had cruelly decided to assign homework on the first day. He had an essay to write for English and a chapter to read for History along with end of chapter questions to go through. It took several hours, but once he was done with all of that, he looked over the worksheet he'd been given in Chemistry. He soon realized he couldn't fill out half the sheet because he'd missed a demonstration at the beginning of class. Fortunately, Lewis owned a chemistry kit that he'd received for his birthday two years ago. He had everything he needed to do the missed experiment on his own.

"Such primitive science," mused Mr. Gray as Lewis began setting everything up.

He measured out an ounce and a half of table salt from the kitchen's shaker and added it to a solution of chemicals he mixed up from his kit. It bubbled furiously for about fifteen seconds before becoming stable. That was all there was to the experiment. Nothing too fancy. With that finished, Lewis was able to finish all the worksheet questions and be done with his homework.

"We leave right now for the party," said Mr. Gray.

"Party?" questioned Lewis. "Kenzie said it was just a small gathering."

Mr. Gray didn't respond. Lewis frowned. He left his chemistry set out as he picked Mr. Gray up and hurried downstairs.

"Snacks first," said Mr. Gray.

Lewis swung by the kitchen, placing Mr. Gray down beside the coffeemaker for a moment to fish out several more sugar cubes. Lewis quickly grabbed a bagel for himself to eat on the go.

"Take twenty dollars," said Mr. Gray, pointing to Lewis's mother's purse. Mr. Gray must have noticed his apprehension. "Don't worry, you put it back later, plus much more."

Lewis quietly opened the purse and slipped a twenty out of the fold of the wallet inside. Both his parents were watching TV down the hall in the living room.

"Good, now be silent. They mustn't know you've gone," said Mr. Gray.

Lewis was anxious about sneaking out. He knew he wouldn't get caught, not with Mr. Gray leading the way, but he wasn't the kind of kid that did bad things. It just felt wrong. He took a bite out of his bagel as he contemplated the possible ramifications of listening to Mr. Gray. Maybe the creature was done hurting people now that Landon was out of the way, and he would simply have a great evening with Kenzie… or something terrible could happen again.

"Go now!" Mr. Gray implored.

Lewis took a deep breath. He picked Mr. Gray up and put him on his shoulders, then slipped out into the night.

CHAPTER

8

Jellybeans

Kenzie lived in the opposite direction as Josie. It was too far to walk, so Lewis grabbed his bicycle, propped up against the side of the house, and balanced Mr. Gray on the handlebars. Melon was outside watching them. A low rumble escaped Mr. Gray's throat—a growl of sorts—directed at the cat. Melon was not perturbed; his tale flicked back and forth as he continued to watch them in silence.

Lewis peddled away.

Sneaking out gave him a bit of a thrill. He'd never purposefully broken the rules before. The evening air felt nice on his face as he peddled faster. Mr. Gray giggled to himself, enjoying the ride as well. They were headed towards the bowl of Edmonds—the most affluent part of town—located in a half-bowl-shaped region where every house had rich views of the Puget Sound. Homes doubled and tripled in value in the span of a block as Lewis crested the top of Pine Street and started down the long hill that stretched nearly all the way to the waterfront.

"No one's going to get hurt tonight, right?" Lewis asked, still apprehensive to be following the creature's directions.

"I wouldn't think so," said Mr. Gray.

The uncertainty was disturbing. "I thought you already knew what was going to happen."

"More or less," said Mr. Gray. "Stop worrying."

Lewis did his best to let go of his nervousness. When they arrived at Kenzie's house, Lewis definitely agreed with Mr. Gray's wording of "party" over Kenzie's description of "small gathering." It looked as if the whole school had turned out for what was inarguably an end of summer rager.

Cars lined every available space on both sides of the street, stretching far up and down the block. Loud music thumped inside the house. Lewis leaned his bike up against the side of the three-car garage and made his way to the front door. More kids were arriving at the same time as him. He recognized several of them from freshman year classes, but he wasn't exactly friendly with any of them. They all approached the front door together.

It opened before anyone could knock. A wasted football player by the name of Jeremy McDonald greeted them. "Beeeer ponnnnng!"

Lewis definitely didn't fit in with the crowd. He went inside anyway.

At sixteen years old, Jeremy was already six-foot-two-inches tall and built like a linebacker. Lewis had never been to any of his school's football games, but it was a safe bet that Jeremy played the position he was clearly born to fill. Jeremy picked up a giant jar of jellybeans that was sitting on a side table in the entryway. "Anyone want to guess how many beans are in here? It's a contest. Put in twenty dollars and you get a guess. The person who's closest wins the jar and the cash."

"That's stupid," said one of the boys that came in with Lewis.

"Four-thousand-two-hundred-ninety-three," said Mr. Gray.

"I'll make a guess," said Lewis. He pulled out his mom's twenty and handed it to Jeremy.

Jeremy slapped him on the back. "My man!" he said as he handed him a pen and a slip of paper.

Lewis filled it out with Mr. Gray's answer. Mr. Gray licked his lips while staring intently at the jellybean jar. Lewis had a sneaking suspicion the creature intended to keep the candy for himself after they won.

Lewis headed deeper into the house looking for Kenzie and eventually found her taking shots with a group of people in the kitchen. "Oh heyyy, you made it!" said Kenzie enthusiastically, her speech slurred. "Guys, this is Lewis, he's new in town."

The other kids in the kitchen looked at each other in confusion but no one corrected Kenzie. More than a few of them had shared classes with Lewis in the past. Lewis shrugged to them when Kenzie glanced away for a second.

"Do you want a shot?" Kenzie asked.

"Say yes," said Mr. Gray.

"Sure," said Lewis, although he very much did not want a shot. The only alcohol that Lewis had ever tried was a sip of his father's beer one time at a family wedding.

Kenzie pushed a full shot glass into his hand. "Yay! On three! One, two…."

Lewis threw it back and instantly gagged at the terrible burning flavor. He tried to swallow, but was pretty sure some of it came back out through his nose. Kenzie didn't seem to notice or care.

"Woo!" she yelled.

"We should play truth or dare!" suggested Ali Cooper, one of Kenzie's cheerleader friends.

"Oh my god," said Kenzie, "that would be so crazy."

"Yeah, so crazy!"

With the girls in agreement, the group in the kitchen migrated over to the living room, nearly doubling in size by the time the impromptu game of truth or dare began.

Suggestions such as "I dare you to sniff my finger" and questions like "how many guys have you kissed" were soon flying back and forth. Lewis managed to dodge having to participate until it was Ali's turn to give out a dare. She pointed at Kenzie. "I dare you to go into the closet with a boy for like five minutes," she said.

"Oh my god, Ali!" said Kenzie. "That's so crazy!"

Kenzie's eyes scanned around the circle until they eventually caught on Lewis. She bit her lip softly as she gazed hazily into his face. "I'll take Lewis," she said. Several kids hooted and hollered rowdily. Lewis was pretty sure his face turned beet red. Kenzie hopped up and stumbled over to him. She reached a hand out and dragged Lewis up onto his feet and led him to the closet at the side of the room. They both stepped inside and Kenzie shut the door behind them.

Lewis could barely see with the small amount of light coming in from under the door, but he could tell Kenzie was looking at him. Her hands were firmly on his hips. Mr. Gray hadn't followed them inside—Lewis was glad of that.

"You have a nice house," Lewis said, awkwardly.

Kenzie giggled. "This isn't my house," she said. Her speech was heavily slurred. "Jeremy McBurger…" she snorted as she laughed openly for a moment. "Jeremy McDonald's dad lives here. He's like on vacation or something." She leaned forward and nuzzled her head into Lewis's neck. Her soft hair felt nice. Lewis's nerves began to ease.

Soon Kenzie had her whole body pressed up against him, grinding with ungentle motions. Excitement began to grow inside Lewis, soon outpacing his nervousness. He felt heavy-handed as he pawed across Kenzie's back in the dark. She craned her neck up. "Aren't you gunna kissss me?" she asked.

A tingling rush of blood flowed to Lewis's cheeks in response. He knew he was blushing. His excitement reached a pinnacle as he leaned in for his first kiss.

He was struck by the acrid scent of bile on Kenzie's breath just before their lips touched. Lewis's nose curled up at the unpleasant odor. Kenzie's lips were soft, but the taste of vomit was on her tongue as she slipped it between Lewis's lips. He felt like he was going to be sick. He pulled away from the kiss and wiped his fingernails across his tongue in the dark.

Kenzie's head drooped and began wobbling strangely. At first Lewis though she was crying from his rejection, but soon he realized she simply couldn't stand up straight. Kenzie toppled over against the coats and ended up on her knees at the bottom of the closet.

Lewis felt terrible. A kiss from Kenzie had been just about his greatest fantasy for the last couple of years, but the disgusting state of her mouth turned his stomach. He bent over to help her back to her feet, but she didn't take his hand. Instead she leaned over onto all fours and began to wretch the alcohol-heavy contents of her stomach out onto the piles of coats she'd knocked down in her fall.

"Cops!" someone yelled from the other side of the closet door.

CHAPTER

9

Along for the Ride

Kenzie was suddenly on her feet, a surge of frightened energy flowing through her. She shoved open the closet door and stumbled out. Lewis spotted Mr. Gray standing off to the side of the room, next to an unattended bowl of potato chips. He appeared to be licking all the flavoring off of them one by one before discarding them back into the same bowl.

"I'm parked down the street," one of Jeremy's more sober friends was saying to him. "Let's just ditch the house and go."

Jeremy glanced around in a panic. Blue and red lights were already pouring in through the front window. He spotted Lewis and Kenzie and gestured for them to join him. "You won, dude," he said, handing Lewis an envelope full of cash. "Spot on with the jellybeans! You wanna get out of here with us?"

"Go with him," said Mr. Gray.

Lewis shrugged. "Sure," he said.

Jeremy, holding the jar of jellybeans, fled with his friend and another girl out the side door. Lewis helped Kenzie along behind them as they all made their way to Jeremy's friend's car.

He gave his bicycle a glance as he passed it by.

"Leave it," said Mr. Gray. "You pick it up later."

Kids were running all over the place, trying to get away before the police could bust them. Lewis just focused on getting Kenzie to put one foot in front of the other. Soon they were inside the car. Lewis was squished in the backseat between Kenzie and Jeremy with the jar of jellybeans. Mr. Gray curled up at his feet. Lewis did his best not to step on him. Everyone was breathing heavily.

"These are my friends—Andrew and Kiera," said Jeremy. They exchanged pleasantries with Lewis. "Oh yeah," said Jeremy. "These are yours too." He handed Lewis the jellybean jar.

Lewis unscrewed the top immediately and threw some into his mouth to clear the taste of Kenzie's kiss away.

"Drop one," said Mr. Gray.

Lewis grabbed a handful. "Anyone want some?"

Kiera, in the front passenger seat, put her hand back. Lewis placed the handful into Kiera's palm, being sure to drop a few to the floor for Mr. Gray.

Kenzie leaned over towards him, lifting her chin as if she wanted another kiss. Lewis tossed several more jellybeans into his mouth instead, then helped her put on her seatbelt before doing up his own.

"You got the stuff?" Jeremy asked Andrew.

"In the trunk," said Andrew with a grin on his face.

Lewis noticed they were driving back in the direction of his own house. "Where are we going?" he asked.

Andrew and Jeremy both laughed. "Gunna have some fun," Jeremy said.

Andrew started driving really slow. He was looking for a specific house.

"It's further up," said Kiera.

They passed Lewis's house, and started going by the creepy house. Kiera suddenly screamed.

Andrew slammed on the breaks, throwing everyone against their seatbelts. Lewis spilled a bunch of jellybeans—he barely managed to hold onto the jar. Mr. Gray started cramming the fallen morsels into his face as fast as he could.

"Whaat?" Andrew asked, looking back and forth frantically for the cause of Kiera's alarm. "Did I hit something?"

"Someone's in there!" said Kiera, pointing at a second-story window of the creepy house. "They were watching us."

Everyone scanned their eyes across the house. Lewis didn't see anything out of the ordinary.

"Don't be stupid," said Andrew. "Nobody goes in there anymore." He continued driving slowly, shaking his head.

Kiera crossed her arms in a huff. "I know what I saw. Someone was up there."

Andrew laughed to himself. "Gunna make me crash being crazy like that."

Kenzie was leaning hard against the window now. She looked like she might be sick again.

"Hey guys," said Lewis, "Kenzie isn't looking so good."

"We're almost there," said Kiera. "Just a couple more blocks."

Kenzie made a gagging noise.

Andrew slammed on the breaks again. "Not in the car!"

Lewis reached over Kenzie and quickly opened the door. Kenzie immediately drooped over and threw up into the street without even undoing her seatbelt.

"Jesus!" said Andrew. "Did it all make it out?"

It hadn't.

Kenzie sat back up in her seat, giving Andrew an enthusiastic thumbs up. There was vomit on her chin. Everyone stared at her in disgust. She closed the door. "I'm good now," she said.

Andrew was clearly annoyed as he started driving again.

A couple of blocks later, Kiera pointed at Josie's house. "There it is!" she said.

Andrew pulled the car over abruptly, still down the block a little ways. He turned off the engine. "Come on!" he said, hopping out.

Mr. Gray gestured for Lewis to follow Andrew's lead. "Go with them," he said.

Lewis stepped out of the car, being careful not to get any of Kenzie's barf on his shoes. He had a bad feeling about where all of this was headed. Mr. Gray climbed down by himself, the jar of jellybeans clutched between his little arms. Lewis waited to shut the door until the gluttonous creature was clear.

Andrew was around the back of the car getting something out of the trunk. Kiera and Jeremy joined him. Kenzie was still too drunk to do much. She hung heavily on Lewis's arm, wobbling as she tried to stand still.

Andrew, Jeremy and Kiera all ran past Lewis carrying rolls of toilet paper and egg cartons. Lewis really wished he wasn't with them right now. He glared over at Mr. Gray, standing on the curbside next to the jar of jellybeans.

Kenzie, despite her drunkenness, stumbled on ahead, joining in with the other three as they began throwing rolls of toilet paper into the branches of a tall maple tree growing in the middle of Josie's front yard. The tree had an old wooden swing hanging from its branches. It was immediately spider-webbed with toilet paper. Many of the rolls flew high, leaving silent trails behind them—long streamers of paper that arced high into the dark sky like confetti before floating back down to tangle with the branches and dewy leaves. Kenzie's throws were not so graceful—they bounced off the lower branches and fell in lumps to the ground below.

Next came the eggs.

They splattered against the house with wet thuds.

"Here, man," said Jeremy, sharing his carton with Lewis. "Let them fly—have some fun."

Mr. Gray reached out and touched one of the eggs, sitting in the corner of the carton. "This one," he said.

Lewis felt like a terrible person. He picked up the egg, but hesitated.

"Throw it hard," said Mr. Gray.

Lewis *really* didn't want to participate.

"You must!" Mr. Gray yelled forcefully.

Lewis threw the egg.

Crash.

A window shattered.

Lewis's jaw dropped open. He really was a terrible person. He was so surprised by the results of his own actions that he didn't notice everyone else running away, back to the car, as fast as their feet would carry them.

CHAPTER

10

Hard Boiled

The porch light flicked on. Lewis suddenly realized he was all alone with Mr. Gray. A moment later, the front door opened and Josie's grandfather came barreling out. Lewis had hesitated for too long.

"Run!" screeched Mr. Gray. "Run home as fast as you can!"

"What the hell do you think you're doing?" Mr. Mays yelled angrily.

Lewis was ashamed. He resolved to stop listening to Mr. Gray and to just be himself. The old Lewis would never have egged a house. He wouldn't have gotten to kiss Kenzie either, but that wasn't exactly as pleasant an experience as he always imagined it to be.

Lewis didn't attempt to flee as Mr. Mays ran over to him.

"I should call the police!" he said.

"I'm sorry," said Lewis, lowering his head. "I was with some kids. I didn't realize what they were going to do. I'm really sorry about the window. I'll pay for it." He held out the envelope full of winnings from the jellybean contest.

Mr. Mays took the envelope and glanced through it. His eyebrows rose. "That... that should cover it," he said, surprised. "But you better be planning on sticking around to help clean up."

Lewis glanced around for Mr. Gray, but he was nowhere to be found. "Yes, sir," said Lewis.

"Come on then," said Mr. Mays, walking back towards the house. "My name's Richard, by the way."

"I'm Lewis, Lewis Graham. I'm in chemistry with Josie."

"I remember. Now watch your feet around the glass," said Mr. Mays. "Who throws a hard-boiled egg?" He shook his head.

Hard-boiled... that explains a few things.

Josie, dressed in a loose fitting nightshirt and pajama bottoms, was standing halfway down the stairs when Lewis came in. Her hair, damp and slightly wavy from a recent shower, was clipped back behind her left ear, giving Lewis his first unobstructed view of her face. Her full lips, framed between her high cheekbones, were pursed tight with concern. She wore the same wide-eyed expression she'd had in chemistry class. Her almond-shaped eyes grew even wider when she recognized Lewis standing before her. She glanced around, clearly looking to see if Mr. Gray was present, but Lewis was still alone.

Mr. Mays went to retrieve a broom and dust pan. Lewis immediately honed in on Josie. "What do you know?" he asked.

Josie peeked out the shutters by the front door. "You have one of them following you," she said.

Lewis nodded. "His name is Mr. Gray."

"Like Fifty Shades?"

"I guess," said Lewis. "He probably hasn't read that though."

"I would hope not," said Josie. "But they are much more aware of our culture than you might expect."

Mr. Mays returned with a pair of brooms. He handed one over to Lewis and together they began cleaning up the shattered glass and bits of hard-boiled egg from the living room floor. There was a sideboard beneath the broken window. The largest shards of glass had fallen straight down on top of it, knocking over several framed photographs that were arranged there. Lewis carefully picked up the shards one at a time and tossed them into a heavy-duty black trash bag in the center of the room.

He righted one of the photographs. It was a picture of Josie sitting on the wooden swing out front under the maple tree. She looked to be only about nine or ten at the time it was taken, but her deep brown eyes stared back into his soul hauntingly. She wasn't smiling in the photo—with lips slightly parted, her expression was sorrowful in a way that broke his heart to gaze upon. The way the light framed her through the branches gave her a sort of innocent, angelic quality that was captivating to see.

Mr. Mays noticed him looking at the photograph. He came straight over, picked it up, and held it lovingly to his chest.

"Difficult times," he said. "How about you work on sweeping the smaller pieces into a pile."

Lewis stepped away from the sideboard. Josie was still watching him intently from midway up the stairs. The same haunting gaze fell across him. It was even more evocative in person. He shied away from her intensity, focusing instead on the task at hand.

Cleaning up his mess took nearly thirty minutes. Bits of glass had scattered everywhere. Once the bulk of the mess was swept up, Mr. Mays brought out a vacuum cleaner and got to work on the finer shards.

Lewis finally got another moment alone with Josie. He sat down beside her on the stairs. "So, how can you see him?" he asked. "Is it because you're Native?"

"No," said Josie. "That's kinda racist."

Lewis felt his face grow hot again.

"One came to me as a child," she said. "Once one reveals itself to you, you can see their whole species."

Lewis nodded with understanding. "Are there a lot of them around?"

Josie shook her head. "Until today, I hadn't seen any since the night my parents died."

Lewis felt the weight behind those words.

"Be very careful with him," she said. "He wants something from you. If you don't do what he says, bad things might happen, but if you do exactly what he says…."

Worse things might happen.

"Try to find out what he wants. Make sure it's what you want."

Mr. Mays finished vacuuming.

"Would you like my help with the outside?" Lewis asked.

Mr. Mays waved his hand dismissively. "Nah, this happens all the time. I'll just hose it off in the morning."

Lewis felt a pang of sadness for Josie. With all the bullying he'd experience from Landon, he'd at least never had anyone attack his home.

"Hold on a second," said Josie. She ran upstairs and disappeared into what Lewis presumed was her bedroom. She reappeared after a couple of seconds with a book under her arm. "Here," she said, handing it to Lewis.

He glanced at its title: *A Secret History of Parcae.*

He'd have to keep it hidden from Mr. Gray. He tucked it into the waistband of his pants and pulled his shirt over the top of it.

"Read it," said Josie.

"I will," he said. "Thank you."

Stepping out into the chilly night air, Lewis found Mr. Gray waiting for him beside the maple tree. He had a scowl on his tiny face. "I told you to run," he said.

"I know," said Lewis, "I froze up."

"You should have run home," said Mr. Gray. "Now I must go back to the Beyond and see what changes your departure from the path has made. You'll just have to face the consequences of your decisions. I'll be back in the morning for school."

Lewis watched this time as Mr. Gray walked off, over to the other side of the tree, and reached out with his scrawny arms into empty space. It was difficult to see in the dim light, but the air seemed to turn hazy in a small patch. Mr. Gray quickly stepped into the deadened space and vanished from sight. After a few seconds the air returned to normal and Lewis continued his trek home.

CHAPTER

11

Where There's Smoke...

Lewis saw the flashing lights from several blocks away. A fire truck, police car, and several aid cars were sitting outside his home. He ran the final blocks back. His mom saw him first. She was hysterical. Sniffling and sobbing, she ran to Lewis and grabbed him in a deathly tight bear hug. His dad and Jenny were soon by his side as well, looking simultaneously pissed off and relieved. Jenny was holding Melon and everyone was in their pajamas.

"What happened?" Lewis asked, looking up at the charred side of their house.

"There was a fire, baby," his mother said.

"We thought you were dead," said Jenny, "burnt up." Their father smacked her on the shoulder. "What? It's true, we did."

Firemen were just finishing spraying down the house. A hose was running in through their front door. One of the fireman approached Lewis's father.

"Well this is an unusual one," he said, "it looks like this was a chemical fire, caused by the contents of a chemistry set spilling out onto the space heater in this room up here." The fireman pointed to Lewis's room.

His whole family turned to look at him. His face went completely white. Lewis had two simultaneous realizations. First, if he had run straight home like Mr. Gray told him to, he could have prevented the fire, and second, the fire could have been caused by Mr. Gray intentionally as a form of punishment.

"Why didn't any of the fire alarms go off?" Lewis's father asked.

The fireman frowned deeply. "There were no batteries in the one at the top of the stairs or in the room of origin."

Again, Lewis's family stared at him, this time demanding answers. "It wasn't me," he said. "I swear! I've never touched any of the smoke detectors."

"And the chemicals?" asked his father.

Lewis didn't know what to say. That part had been his fault. "I had a chemistry assignment... I forgot to put everything away after. I didn't know this could happen—"

"—Do you have any idea how close we all came to dying?!" his father yelled. "Do you have any idea how much all of this is going to cost? I don't even know if this type of fire is covered by our insurance!"

Lewis's mother put her hand on his dad's shoulder, pulling him back in an attempt to subdue his anger. Lewis was in complete shock. Mr. Gray was unraveling his life. Everyone he knew was potentially in danger if he angered the creature.

"Where were you?" Jenny asked.

Lewis barely even heard the question. His mind was reeling with panic. He was in way over his head. He realized his sister was staring at him. "I was just out with some friends."

Jenny leaned in and smelled his breath. "Oh my god," she said in a whisper. "Were you at McDonald's rager?"

Lewis was glad his parents had stepped too far away to overhear them.

"I was out with Kenzie," he said.

A flash of a smile cracked Jenny's face. "I'm still pissed at you for burning half the house down," she said.

After the police and firemen gathered all the information they needed from Lewis's father, he drove them to a motel on the other side of town. Luckily the car was fine. Apparently the fire was contained to Lewis's room and the upstairs hallway, but the water damage from putting it out reached considerably farther.

Lewis ended up sleeping on the couch of the room his father rented. He laid his head down on his pillow but there was no rest to be had within the spinning funnel of concern that had taken over his mind. He pulled out the book Josie gave him and began to read under his blanket with only his phone to light the pages.

Flipping through, it appeared to read like historical non-fiction, except that it was full of fantastical deviations from standard history. The prologue described the Parcae (singular, Parca) as mischievous gremlins from another plane of existence. They possessed abilities far beyond what mankind was conventionally capable of comprehending. Parcae, when in their natural realm known as the Beyond, could see the future and travel through time. Some people, which the book referred to as the Chosen, had multiple potential fates, and the Parcae could see all of them at once. Guiding the Chosen seemed to be a favorite pastime of the Parcae. The Chosen could be nudged from one fate to another by a Parca's meddling. The whole book was full of examples of such meddling from all throughout human history.

As Lewis read on, he took special note in one passage in particular which said that major changes in a Chosen's fate were always up to the decisions of that individual, and *not* the Parcae. The Parcae could never make the decisions for them—only guide them towards a path.

Just as Josie described, the book mentioned that a person could only see the Parcae species if one revealed itself to them.

Lewis turned back to the cover and then through the opening pages again. There was no author or publisher information listed. The book felt old, but flipping through, he saw that the timeline of described events had sections about modern times and even times yet to come, reaching far into the future. Strangely, the sections were not in chronological order—at least not as humans experience time.

There were passages on many major world events. Lewis pauses briefly on a section about World War II. Hitler was apparently one of the Chosen. A Parca guided him to kill many other Chosen at that time. The war marked a major shift in the ultimate path of humanity.

Continuing on, he found a section on the death of Christ to be of considerable interest. He recognized the name Longinus on the page—that's what Mr. Gray said his name was earlier that morning when they first met. According to the text, Longinus was responsible for directing a Roman soldier to stab Jesus with the Spear of Destiny. Jesus, interestingly, was not one of the Chosen. His destiny was set from the beginning, until one of the Chosen changed it for him by making him a martyr with a spear to the side.

If Lewis was to believe the book, small nudges here and there had led to history, as everyone knew it, coming to pass. It was mindboggling and somewhat terrifying to think about. The results of the various changes did not adhere to any particular pattern that Lewis could recognize. Some passages denoted terrible events and tragedies such as wars sparked by tiny shifts in fate, while others contained great human successes and triumphs. Morally speaking, the Parcae were all over the place. The most unsettling part was that he still had no idea what it all was leading up to.

He read on until exhaustion overtook him.

CHAPTER

12

Ultimate Fate

Lewis awoke to find Mr. Gray opening packets of sugar in the coffee condiments area.

"I prefer the cubes," he said.

Lewis couldn't respond with his family present, but he continued to watch Mr. Gray out of the corner of his eye while he ate breakfast. No one spoke. His family was still very upset with him for the role his negligence played in the fire. Lewis's father drove him and Jenny to school once they were finished eating. He'd taken the day off from work to focus on figuring out what was to happen next to get the house fixed. He handed each of his children some money as they got out of the car— they were to ride the metro bus back after school. They would be spending a lot of time at the motel while a construction crew assessed the damage and got started on the restoration.

With a little bit of extra time before class, Lewis headed straight to the nearest restroom. He was looking for an empty place to confront Mr. Gray. He peeked his head in.

Empty.

He sat down in the largest stall and placed his backpack, containing Mr. Gray, in his lap.

"I'm one of the Chosen, aren't I?" he asked.

If Mr. Gray was surprised at the question he didn't show it. "You are," he said. "I told you, you are important later."

"So my destiny isn't decided?"

"You have several possibilities," said Mr. Gray. "Most are not good."

Lewis took a breath to settle his nerves. "And you are nudging me towards a good path?"

"I am nudging you towards the only path that doesn't end in disaster for your race."

Lewis narrowed his eyes. "So, what? If I don't listen to you the world's gunna explode?"

"Not explode," said Mr. Gray. "Your realm will be snipped from existence. Erased. The energy will be repurposed by the Agares."

Lewis's jaw dropped open. It was difficult to take anything Mr. Gray said at face value since he didn't trust him, but it seemed too extreme a lie to make up. "Who or what are the Agares?"

"Another race," said Mr. Gray. "They are parasitic. Outgrew their own realm."

"Ok…" said Lewis. "So—?"

"—I already know all of your questions," interrupted Mr. Gray, losing his patience. "There is a war raging amongst the immortals. It is being fought in the Beyond, within your realm, and throughout many others. Some of my kind are working with the Agares to end your realm, others, like me, want to save it. It is a bad trend, repurposing timelines the way they do. It causes unbalance. I do not believe they will stop, even after all of the realms are snipped. I enjoy humanity. It is very important that you do everything I say. Your world's ultimate fate lies in the balance."

Lewis opened his mouth to ask one more question.

"No," said Mr. Gray, "I can't tell you your possible fates nor can I tell you what your pinnacle decisions will be. That would be cheating. I won't say anymore. You overthink things if I do."

Lewis had a lot to process.

The door to the bathroom opened as another student came in.

"I'm going to nap now," said Mr. Gray. "You can be quite exhausting."

Trust

Lewis headed to class with Mr. Gray curled up at the bottom of his backpack like a sleeping cat. The high school's schedule had students take six classes each semester—three one day, then the other three the next, so Lewis proceeded to second-year French with Madam Defour. Lewis wasn't a fan of French class. He wished he'd just picked Spanish like most of the other students his freshman year, but it was too late for that now. He'd heard at the end of middle school that Kenzie was going to take French, which was his primary reason for signing up. Unfortunately, there were two French teachers, and Lewis and Kenzie ended up in different classes freshman year.

Lewis had Madam Defour last year as well. She was strict and a harsh grader. Like most language classes, no English was to be spoken. Anyone caught breaking that rule was immediately docked participation points for the day.

He passed Jeremy McDonald chatting with Kiera in the hallway. Jeremy spotted him as well and slapped him on the back. "Hey, man," he said, "did you get caught? We all ran different directions but no one saw you again after we got back to the car."

"No," Lewis lied. "I just ran home. I don't live too far from there."

"Ah, cool, was worried you got busted."

Andrew came walking over to talk to Jeremy. His left eye had a terrible shiner as if someone had punched him in the face. He scowled when he saw Lewis, and then pointedly ignored his presence.

Lewis made a questioning gesture towards Andrew, confused by the attitude he was receiving. Andrew flinched away from the movement. Lewis remained genuinely confused at the wordless exchange as he headed into class.

After his evening with Kenzie, Lewis wasn't exactly thrilled to see that she was in Madam Defour's class this year too. She sat beside him and spent the whole class whispering in his ear, asking stupid questions every five seconds about what was going on.

Did she even pay attention during first year?

It was extremely irritating, especially when Madam Defour overheard her and docked them both points for the day.

"But I wasn't even speaking English!" Lewis protested in English.

"Parle Français *[Speak French]*," Madam Defour demanded, docking him an extra point.

Lewis wished Mr. Gray would do something mean to her. He was still asleep in Lewis's backpack, snoring loudly.

Madam Defour had everyone introduce themselves to the class. They were supposed to say their names and a fun fact about their summer.

On Kenzie's turn, she said: "Jerma pell Kenzie— *[gibberish Kenzie—]*"

"Je m'appelle, *[I call myself,]*" corrected Madam Defour.

"And um…" Kenzie continued unperturbed, "je voudrais um… cheer camp mes amis. Tres bon. *[I want um… cheer camp my friends. Very good.]*"

Madam Defour stared at her for a moment before moving on. She was probably contemplating whether or not it was worth the risk failing Kenzie and possibly having to see her again the following year if she landed back in her class again.

Kenzie proceeded to copy every answer off of Lewis's worksheet and then excuse herself to the bathroom for nearly fifteen minutes.

After French was over, Lewis headed to the locker room to get ready for Physical Education with Coach Phillips. PE beat out French for top slot on Lewis's least favorite class list. This was mainly because of all the bullying and awkward social interaction he was forced to endure in gym classes in the past. He also wasn't particularly athletic, which made running the pacer test on day one all the more humiliating.

He changed into shorts in the locker room as flashbacks of abuse from Landon drifted across his mind. He'd been pantsed while changing in middle school. This was before he'd even started puberty. Kids made fun of him behind his back every day after that. Landon made fun of him to his face. He was glad Landon was still out of school from the accident.

Maybe he did deserve it like Mr. Gray said after all, Lewis mused.

He left his backpack, along with a sleeping Mr. Gray, in his locker, and padlocked it shut.

The dreaded pacer test was the first thing on the docket for the day. Lewis spotted Josie as everyone lined up to run half the length of the gym and back at decreasing time intervals. Anyone that didn't make it back before the beep sounded was finished and their score recorded.

Josie's t-shirt was tied with a knot in the front, exposing some caramel-smooth midriff that Lewis found himself staring at as the pacer test began. It wasn't strictly to dress code, but Coach Phillips didn't call her on it. Everyone dashed ahead of him, but he was quick to make up the time. The first round was easy enough. He made it back well before the beep. Josie's shorts were tight and showed off her butt. She had lean, muscular legs—long and creamy brown. Her silky hair was tied back in a ponytail that bounced out behind her as the next round began. Lewis found himself following behind Josie, enjoying the view of her backside as she sprinted across the gym.

She turned at the line and immediately collided with Lewis. They both tumbled to the gym floor. It was completely Lewis's fault. Josie wore an annoyed expression as the beep sounded and they were the first two people out of the race.

Coach Phillips didn't care that a collision knocked them out rather than their own physical limitations. It wasn't a good start for their grades.

Josie and Lewis sat down beside one another against the wall of the gym to wait for the rest of the students to finish.

"I read a bunch of the book," said Lewis.

Josie grunted in affirmation, still annoyed.

"And I talked to him this morning. He told me about a war between the Parcae. Apparently, our whole world could end if the wrong side wins."

"Let me guess," said Josie. "He says he's one of the good ones?"

Lewis wrinkled his nose. "Well, yes," he said.

"He'd hardly tell you if he was a bad one, don't you think?"

"I guess not."

"Look," said Josie, turning to face him, "when I was nine, one of them began to visit me. She would tell me everything I needed to hear to complete the little tasks she gave me, and in the end my dad flipped our car and he died. And my mom died. And I was all alone bleeding in the street." Her eyes were hard as steel. "She didn't tell me that was going to happen—that everyone I loved would be taken from me. She didn't tell me where it was all leading. She made it sound like we were having fun, leading to something grand where I would be happy. She actually had me undo my seatbelt and stand on the backseat. I flew right through the windshield. She told me I would have died too had I not listened, but I know she could have prevented the whole thing if she wanted to."

Lewis didn't know what to say. Her apprehension of Mr. Gray made total sense.

"That was the last night I saw her. I never learned why she came to me, and for a while I even began to think maybe I made it all up."

Lewis placed his hand on Josie's shoulder. He could feel the heat of her skin through her t-shirt. "I'm really sorry," he said.

Josie slumped back against the wall, looking defeated. She leaned her head over onto Lewis's shoulder. An electric tingle ran up his arm. "I just don't want to see you get hurt," she whispered. Still lying against him, she tilted her chin up, so that she could see his face. "There are so many things I want to tell you.…"

Lewis's heart began to beat faster. The intimate position felt natural as she stared up into his eyes. "Then tell me," he said. "I want to know everything. Mr. Gray says my decisions will save or end humanity. I need to know everything." There was no way of knowing whether or not he could trust Mr. Gray. The Parca that came to Josie wasn't the same one, and though it had led her astray, Lewis didn't like to judge an entire people by the actions of one. That said, it was certainly an ominous cautionary tale.

Josie closed her eyes, in thought, and took several deep breaths. "Not here," she said. When she opened them again they were glistening with moisture, looking like molten drops of chocolate.

She sat up suddenly, lifting her head from Lewis's arm. He felt the absence, as if she'd taken something away from him. It was an odd sensation.

"After school," she said, "if you can ditch Mr. Gray, come to the wooded area on the other side of the field. I'll wait for you there."

They rejoined the rest of the class. Lewis began to count down the minutes until they could talk again.

CHAPTER

14

The Cure for a Broken Heart

Upon returning to his locker Lewis heard Mr. Gray's muffled cries. He undid the lock and opened the door to find Mr. Gray already out of the backpack. All of Lewis's books and school supplies were strewn about the bottom of the locker.

"I was stuck," said Mr. Gray.

"I thought you could just open a portal or something," said Lewis.

"I can only open doors in weak spots," he said.

Mr. Gray hopped out of the locker with a pouty scowl on his face. He followed Lewis on foot to lunch after Lewis finished repacking his bag. Lewis bought a turkey sandwich from the deli and made his way into the cafeteria. Kenzie spotted him from across the way and waved.

"Sit by Kenzie," said Mr. Gray.

Lewis was feeling disillusioned to the wonders of Kenzie. "Do I have to?" he asked.

"Do you want to get snipped?"

Lewis headed over to Kenzie. "Heyyy," said Kenzie. "Madam Defour is *SUCH* a drag."

"Always agree," said Mr. Gray with a smile. "You know."

"I know," said Lewis to both of them at once.

"She's like, 'parlay frech-swa'. I mean how rude is that?!"

"Mhm," said Lewis as he sat down beside her.

Kenzie leaned in close and whispered in his ear. "I didn't get all I wanted earlier."

Lewis raised an eyebrow.

Kenzie dove in with an unexpected kiss. It definitely caught Lewis by surprise. He chocked slightly on his own spit and almost fell off the end of the bench seat as she smushed her face against his. It wasn't disgusting like the night before, but it was hard to enjoy kissing her when every fiber of her being had grown to annoy him.

Lewis, eyes still open as Kenzie prodded at his clenched teeth with her tongue, spotted Landon walking into the cafeteria. His arm was in a sling and he was glaring around back and forth as if searching for someone. Lewis hadn't expected to see him back in school so soon.

He didn't wish to solicit anymore hate from Landon for being around Kenzie, especially since he wasn't enjoying the experience. He immediately coughed into Kenzie's mouth to make her pull away from the kiss.

He leaned around Kenzie to see if Landon had spotted him yet and found the bully glaring directly at him.

So much for not pissing him off....

Lewis braced himself for a confrontation. Landon stared him down for a good ten seconds, but then walked away without so much as a word. Lewis wondered if perhaps Landon hadn't seen the kiss after all. The intimidating stare could have just been Landon's response to him being next to Kenzie. Lewis wasn't usually that lucky, but he was following Mr. Gray's instructions, so maybe it would all work out for the best.

Mr. Gray was staring at Lewis now as well. "You don't have to put up with Kenzie anymore," he said. "Her part towards your destiny is played out."

Lewis blinked several times. He was beyond confused. Mr. Gray had been pushing him towards Kenzie hard since he first appeared. *And now he's just done?* It didn't make any sense— nothing had even happened. *All he's done is make her like me by having me agree to all the stupid things she says, and now her part is just 'played out'?*

Lewis pretended to tie his shoe so he could lean under the table and have a word with his little troublemaker. "What do you mean she's played out?" he whispered.

"Exactly what it sounds like," said Mr. Gray. "You're done with her—finished—you can kick her to the curb—her destiny lies elsewhere," Mr. Gray waved his hand as if saying something mystical. "She is horribly annoying."

"I know," said Lewis. "But why did you even have me going for her in the first place if you're just going to have me end it now?"

"You don't need to end it," said Mr. Gray, "just ghost her."

Lewis blinked several more times. He sat back up. "I have to go," he said.

"Whaat?" asked Kenzie.

Lewis stood up and walked away.

"Ok! See you later," said Kenzie.

Mr. Gray hustled to catch up to Lewis as he exited the cafeteria.

Lewis finished his sandwich while on the move to his last class of the day—math. He sat down outside the classroom and waited for lunch to end. Mr. Gray crawled into the opening of a nearby vending machine and retrieved several candy bars. After crawling back out, he silently handed one over to Lewis.

"Chocolate helps with heartbreak," said Mr. Gray before laughing hysterically.

Lewis definitely wasn't heartbroken. He unwrapped the bar and took a bite. "Good riddance," he said with his mouth full. The turn from practically obsessing over Kenzie to despising her presence had been sharp. Lewis figured that had been Mr. Gray's intention all along. He couldn't imagine how his disillusionment to the wonders of Kenzie would ultimately change his future. Even less so, he had no idea how anything that had happened in the last day could possibly lead to him saving humanity from the Agares.

Math went by without a hitch. Mr. Gray spouted the answers to all the problems on Lewis's worksheet so that he wouldn't have any homework later. Lewis still didn't trust him, but he was enjoying him more now that he wasn't being asked to do anything uncomfortable.

After school he met Jenny at the metro bus stop and informed her that he wouldn't be riding back to the motel with her.

"Why not?" she asked.

"I'm going to walk back. I just need to clear my head."

"That's like three miles," said Jenny. "Whatever. I'll see ya later."

Lewis headed towards the field to meet with Josie. Mr. Gray was still following on his heels. "I really would like to be alone for a while," Lewis said to him.

"Fine," said Mr. Gray, "hurry back, though. There is much we need to do tonight." He quickly stepped over to a bush and opened a portal to the Beyond.

Once Lewis was certain Mr. Gray was completely gone he continued on to the other side of the field.

CHAPTER

15

A Flash of Blue

Lewis hurried to meet with Josie. He couldn't be sure how long Mr. Gray would leave him unattended. He still had so many questions he wanted to ask Josie. As he entered the small greenbelt beside the field he could hear Josie talking to somebody. It was a boy, although he couldn't see who it was through the trees.

"You have no choice, it has to happen," said the boy.

Josie made a frustrated whining sound.

Lewis ducked through the brush. By the time he was at Josie's side all he saw was a flash of blue as the boy ran out the other side of the greenbelt and disappeared.

Josie looked shaken as she turned around. "Lewis!"

"Who was that?" he asked.

"Nothing," said Josie, not realizing her answer didn't fit the question. "So how are things with Kenzie?" She was trying to change the subject. Lewis thought he detected a hint of jealousy in her voice.

He gave a half-shrug. "I really liked her for a long time, but now that I'm in it, it just doesn't feel right. I'm not even sure what I thought I saw in her to begin with if I'm being totally honest. I don't even know what I want anymore."

Josie's focus shifted back and forth between Lewis's eyes as he spoke.

"You know, it's kinda funny," he continued, "when Mr. Gray first appeared I asked him what he wanted and he said the real question was what I wanted. I thought I knew, but I guess I don't." Lewis crossed his arms. "Except I know I want the truth."

Josie's mouth pinched up. She had sad eyes.

"So are you going to tell me who that was, or…." Lewis didn't hear the footsteps approaching in the soft soil behind him until it was too late.

He spun around just as Andrew with his black eye slammed into his chest. Lewis hit the ground hard sending the wind rushing out of him. Josie screamed. Jeremy and Landon were there as well. Jeremy quickly grabbed Josie around the middle. He pinned her arms to her sides as she kicked out and screamed again, trying to struggle free. He was easily twice her size.

Landon glared at Lewis in silence.

Enraged, Lewis turned back towards Jeremy and Josie.

"We know what you did," Jeremy said to Lewis. He wrenched Josie around several times trying to subdue her struggling.

Andrew dragged Lewis up and shoved him against the trunk of a tree. He pressed his forearm firmly to Lewis's neck. He could barely breathe.

"I told you to stay away from Kenzie," said Landon. He punched Lewis hard in the stomach with his non-injured arm. Andrew pushed even harder on Lewis's throat as he cried out in pain.

Jeremy held his hand over Josie's mouth, muffling her cries. Lewis directed a hateful glare at Jeremy as Landon placed several more gut wrenching punches against his abdomen.

"You can have Kenzie!" Lewis cried out. "I don't even like her anymore!"

"No kidding," said Landon. "Too late, though."

Lewis felt like he was going to vomit as the attack continued. His body felt like a bruised banana as he fell to the dirt. Landon and Andrew began using their feet, kicking Lewis repeatedly all over. He tried to block their blows, clenching up into a ball, but each kick still felt like he was being hit with a sledge hammer.

All he could hear was the grunts of his attackers as they ruthlessly beat him, and the heart wrenching whimpers of Josie through Jeremy's smothering palm.

Blood filled Lewis's mouth. The metallic taste was thick on his tongue. A blow to the head made his vision shake. Blotches of darkness filled his mind. There was nothing he could do. The pain was too much. The last thing he thought he heard as he slipped from consciousness was the wiry cry of Mr. Gray yelling: "Stop!"

Everything went dark in the blur of the torment.

CHAPTER

16

Bad News

A persistent beeping roused Lewis from his slumber. His mind was hazy, wondering between thoughts of jellybeans and hard boiled eggs. He was sore beyond belief, barely able to move as he peeked open his eyelids—they were ladened with a heavy layer of crust that made it impossible to see past a general blur.

Josie!

He suddenly recalled his beating.

Remembering the look of terror in Josie's eyes filled Lewis with rage.

The beeping sounds grew closer together. He rubbed his eyes with his fingers, determined to see.

"He's waking up!" said Jenny's voice from somewhere nearby.

Rustling sounded as several people stood up from chairs.

"Can you hear me, baby?" asked his mother.

He felt her fingers caressing his greasy hair. When he finally managed to open his eyes fully, he found his father there as well, a hardened scowl tight on his face. Mr. Gray was present too, sitting patiently on the window ledge. He glanced over at Lewis but said nothing as his family closed in on him.

"Do you know what happened?" asked his father.

Lewis began to nod, but the motion made his neck pinch. All of his muscles were clenched up tight like balls of barbed wire.

"Your friend brought you here," his mother cooed. "She was at your side for hours."

"Just left a little while ago," said Jenny. Lewis knew it was Josie from Jenny's disapproving frown.

"We should press chargers on those boys," said his father.

"Was it Landon?" Jenny asked.

"Yeah," said Lewis. His voice was full of gravel. "And a couple of other jocks."

"Landon?" questioned his mother. "I thought you two were friends?"

"Not for years, mom," said Jenny.

Lewis grimaced.

"I don't understand… he was always such a kind boy…."

Lewis's mother was a bit out of touch with his reality.

"We should let him rest," said his father. He stepped out of the room to talk to one of the nurses.

His mother wore a sorrowful frown. She kissed him gently on the forehead before following his father out of the room. "I'll get you some food, honey," she said.

Jenny gave a meek wave before departing as well.

Mr. Gray hopped down from the window ledge where he'd been waiting for his turn with Lewis. He did not look pleased. "You've thrown everything off, straying from your path like this," he said. "I really wish you would listen to me. It's vital you do exactly as I say from now on or some particularly unsavory things start happening."

It sounded like a threat.

"Josie is bad news," Mr. Gray continued. "Things get complicated around her. You shouldn't see her anymore."

Lewis felt beaten down in every way imaginable. He knew in his heart that if the fate of the world relied upon him staying away from Josie, everyone was screwed.

"You're boring for a while," said Mr. Gray. "No decisions to make." He hopped down from the chair he was standing on and made his way to the corner of the room. The deadened space of a portal opened up in front of him. "I'll be back when you need me," he said before stepping through.

Over the next couple of weeks, Mr. Gray visited him occasionally, but he didn't garner any advice, he was simply there to eat Lewis's jello, brought to him with his meals from time to time by the nursing staff.

Landon and Andrew had nearly killed him. A concussion caused swelling in Lewis's brain, forcing him to remain in the hospital much longer than he would have liked. The days were boring. Other than his family, no one came to visit. Lewis wished Josie would return, but she never came back. Lewis felt worse for her than he did for himself. She had experienced too much trauma in her life already. He couldn't imagine how it must have felt for her, watching helplessly, filled with fear as he was beaten half to death in front of her eyes.

Lewis felt like he owed her, and not just for bringing him to the hospital. He owed her a debt for the added trauma he'd brought to her life.

On the day Lewis was finally discharged from the hospital, he already knew the first person he was going to visit. He would not be heeding Mr. Gray's advice.

CHAPTER

17

Fate Is What You Make It

During Lewis's time in the hospital a construction team worked fast on the water, smoke, and fire damage to the Graham family's house. The work wasn't complete yet, but they had progressed far enough that Lewis and his family were able to move back in. Lewis's room was still a disaster zone. His dad set up a blowup mattress for him in the living room.

Lewis plopped down on the mattress, testing it out. It was too firm at the moment, but it was still better than a hospital bed. He knew it would deflate slowly throughout the night, anyway. Having just concluded their first family dinner in forever, Lewis's dad was making himself an after-dinner coffee.

His father made an exasperated sigh. "Who used all the sugar?" he asked.

"Don't look at me," said Jenny.

"I've only been home an hour," said Lewis. *Mr. Gray must have stopped by for a snack.*

92

"Maybe the construction workers have been using it," said his mother.

His dad sipped his coffee, black, and made a face. He'd been grumpy a lot recently. Lewis felt bad for adding to his stress a lot since Mr. Gray first appeared. He took one more sip then walked straight to the kitchen and poured the whole cup down the drain. "I'm going to bed," he said. It was seven o'clock.

Reunited with *A Secret History of Parcae*, Lewis was finally able to read some more while he waited for the rest of his family to turn in for the night. He hoped to glean a little bit more about the way the Parcae did their manipulation. *How likely is it that Mr. Gray is lying to me?* The Parcae seemed to follow a loose set of rules for dealing out their guidance: They couldn't tell their subject what their destiny was or what choices would lead to major changes in their fate. They couldn't change the fate of a non-Chosen individual directly, but they could indirectly change anyone's destiny by leading a Chosen down a different path. Hitler was a good example of that.

The Parcae weren't supposed to reveal themselves to non-Chosen people, although that rule was sometimes broken in order to prove a point to a Chosen. One Parca in particular named Mendacius had on many occasions revealed himself to non-Chosen to scare them, just for fun. He was eventually punished for his antics, but not before scaring people into believing in ghosts and demons all across the mortal timeline.

There were some notes about the Agares as well—the species that Mr. Gray claimed was trying to snip humanity from existence. Being inter-dimensional like the Parcae, they'd gathered various creatures from other realms that were of use to them. Within their ranks fought shapeshifters, giants, vampiric ghasts, fear-inducing empaths called dreadnaughts, and many other terrors that formed the roots of dozens of the most horrifying myths and legends known to mankind. The text had a picture of what appeared to be a bearded, pointy-faced old man riding a crocodile. According to the caption, the Agares' reptilian mounts were something like the mythical basilisk. They had the ability to temporarily freeze the passage of time with their mere presence.

Notably, the Parcae were not affected by the basilisks. It had something to do with them coming from the Beyond and not truly being part of the stream of time that the basilisks were freezing.

The Agares were described as Mr. Gray had purported. They wanted to repurpose the energy that the various realms ran on. The only thing standing in their way was the unpredictable nature of the Chosen.

After about an hour, Lewis's mom went to bed early. Jenny went up to her room as well, leaving Lewis to make his escape.

He wasn't being directed by Mr. Gray this time. His ribs were still bruised and sore. He had to move slowly to avoid wincing in pain as he got up from the air mattress. Every step was a trial of will. He took out a blue hoodie from a box of old clothing his mom had retrieved for him from out of the attic. It was worn out, but he didn't have much of a selection when it came to autumn clothing. The fire had taken his whole wardrobe. He pulled it on gently over his head and tip-toed over to the side door.

It barely made a sound as it clicked open. Lewis slipped out into the night. He'd never retrieved his bicycle from Jeremy's house—not that he would have been able to ride it with the state his ribs were in. He set out on foot to Josie's house.

He eyed the creepy house suspiciously as he passed. The halfway boarded-up windows always made him feel like he was being watched. He shook it off and continued towards Josie's.

His mind wandered to the earthy scent of her hair—he'd gotten a whiff of it when she'd laid her head on him in gym class. It smelled like standing in the forest just after a hard rain. Little puddles filling in his footprints; the water still rippling as droplets fell from the glistening leaves overheard. Saturated earth. It was like a memory, but not of any specific time. It was funny how a smell could do that—even just the memory of a smell. Such a vivid experience all tied up into a neat little bundle like a universal truth; nostalgia. He missed the essence of Josie, though admittedly, he barely even knew her. Still, he felt drawn to her.

When he got to Josie's street, a wave of panic rushed over him: A police car was sitting outside her house. After coming home to the fire, an emergency vehicle outside of his destination was a triggering sight. An officer was just saying goodbye to Mr. Mays as Lewis ran up. The officer eyed Lewis suspiciously.

Mr. Mays waved the cop off. "Hello, Lewis," he said, a grim expression on his face.

"Is everything okay?" he asked.

Mr. Mays shook his head. The worried knot in Lewis's chest clenched harder.

"Come in," said Mr. Mays, "I'll explain."

Lewis stepped into the silent house, a sense of dread enveloping him.

"Josie's gone missing," said Mr. Mays. "A note was left, but… it's easier to show you." He led Lewis upstairs to Josie's room.

The first thing Lewis noticed before he even entered was the overturned desk chair and unusual clutter all across the floor. It wasn't the normal mess of a teenage girl's room—there had been a struggle.

"Don't touch anything," Mr. Mays warned as Lewis stepped into the room.

Lewis stepped gingerly around the mess surveying everything for anything that would tell him more about what had happened. He found blood smeared on Josie's bedding and pillow—a lot of blood. His heart sank even further.

"Here," said Mr. Mays from behind him.

Lewis turned around to see him pointing at the wall beside the door. A message was scrawled in blood: "Fate is what you make it." He had no idea what to make of it. He'd seen enough. He stepped carefully back out of the room.

"Is there anything you can tell me," asked Mr. Mays.

Lewis shook his head. "I've been in the hospital for weeks," he said. "I haven't seen Josie since…." *This couldn't be Landon, could it?* It was a worrisome thought. He hadn't expected Landon to be capable of nearly killing him, and yet…. *What else might he do for revenge?*

"Since?" asked Mr. Mays.

"Since before I was in the hospital," said Lewis. "I'm sorry, I have to go. If I hear anything, you'll be the first one to know." He ran back down the stairs and out the front door. He wasn't sure if the idea that Landon could be involved with Josie's disappearance was ridiculous or not. He didn't want to say anything to anyone just yet—not without any evidence. He needed to see Landon himself and get a read on him.

Mr. Gray was waiting for him when he got to the end of the driveway. "You can never leave well enough alone," he said.

CHAPTER

18

Sacrifice

Lewis needed to question Mr. Gray, but a police cruiser was approaching from down the street. It drove by slowly with its spotlight on, shining back and forth on either side of the road. The manhunt was already underway for Josie. The light stopped on Lewis and Mr. Gray for a moment before the window of the cruiser rolled down.

"Are you coming from the Mays household?" the officer asked.

"Yes, sir," said Lewis. "I've just heard about Josie…."

"Hurry home," said the officer. "If you learn anything about Josie, be sure to call the police. Maybe ask around to any mutual friends as well—anywhere she might have run off to."

Josie didn't run away. "Yes, sir," said Lewis. The cruiser continued on down the street.

"They don't find her," said Mr. Gray.

He immediately peppered Mr. Gray with questions: "What's happened to Josie?? Is she okay? Does Landon have her?"

Mr. Gray put his hands on his hips. "I told you to stay away from her," he said. "No, Landon doesn't have her, but as far as if she's alright, no, probably not, though I can only guess at her fate."

"What do you mean you don't know?! You know everyone's fate!"

"Not everyone's," said Mr. Gray. "I know some of her potential fates, but as for which path she happens to be on at the moment, I cannot say. She is Chosen, like you."

Josie being Chosen explained why a Parca had come to her as a child, but it didn't answer Lewis's more pressing questions. "Well then what is her most likely fate?" he asked.

"You know I can't tell you things like that—it would be breaking the rules."

"Then where is she right now?! You don't have to tell me the future to tell me that!"

Mr. Gray pursed his thin lips. "Most likely the Agares or one of their agents has taken her," he said. "Parcae are not the only ones who visit the mortal plane. Josie has probably been taken for sacrifice. It is difficult for me to even guess at her future. I told you to stay away from her—I told you this because when those whose destinies are not certain interact, the effects are entirely unforeseeable—billions of possible variations. I do not know Josie's future. I am certain, though, that if she was taken by the Agares, it was because of that very reason. If all the Chosen are snipped from the timeline, the future becomes fixed. Right now, that would mean the end of humanity and the entire mortal realm."

"What do we do?" Lewis asked. "We have to save her!"

Mr. Gray shook his tiny head. "There is nothing we can do. She is beyond either of our reaches now. You must stay focused on your own path. The time draws near for you to make your own pinnacle decision. I cannot tell you what it is, but I trust you will make the right choice when the time comes." Mr. Gray gave Lewis one last sideways look as he began to walk away from him. "And you better make the right choice, for your world's sake."

Lewis was frustrated beyond words. He wanted to cry or scream, or kick the stupid creature so hard he flew clear across the street.

"No pressure!" quipped Mr. Gray before vanishing once again into his own realm.

CHAPTER

19

Fated

Lewis ran all the way home ignoring the pain in his ribs, made worse by every jarring footfall. If Mr. Gray wasn't going to help him, the only thing he had left to consult was the book Josie gave him. He hadn't finished reading through its pages yet, having not had it with him in the hospital, and so could only hope that there might be something of use to him in one of the passages. Perhaps there was more about the Agares or… he didn't know what, but it was the only hope he had left. He clung to it like a life raft in a sea of despair.

He snuck back in the side door and found the book right where he left it beside the air mattress. He sat down on the couch and read until there were no more words left to read. There was no more mention of the Agares. He flipped back through and reread the section about them that he'd already seen. Nothing new stood out to him. The Agares saw life from all the other realms as inferior to their own. To them, snipping Lewis's world would be like steamrolling over an anthill to make room for condominiums. There was no reasoning with something like that—they wouldn't care to listen.

Lewis reread some of the earlier passages, making sure he hadn't missed anything. An hour later, he knew for sure that the book wasn't going to aid him in finding Josie. It was disheartening, to say the least.

A reflection of light shined across the wall, coming in through the dining room window. Lewis assumed it was a passing car at first, but it didn't move smoothly enough. It danced back and forth until Lewis got up to investigate. He stared out the window into the darkness searching for the source.

Across the street, masked in shadow, a hooded figure was holding up a small round mirror—perhaps from a makeup compact—and reflecting the light from a nearby lamp into his window.

Josie?

Lewis tossed *A Secret History of Parcae* down on the air mattress as he made his way to the side door and snuck out once again. He ran around the house and out into his front yard. The figure was gone. He stepped into the street and strained his eyes in the darkness as he searched back and forth for the mysterious individual.

A blur of motion moving away from him in the distance caught his eye, back in the direction of Josie's house. Lewis chased after it but quickly lost sight. His heart was pounding in his eardrums as he neared the creepy house. He glanced over at the structure just as lantern light flashed out through one of the downstairs windows.

An unsettling feeling began to gnaw at the lining of Lewis's stomach. He approached the house quietly, glancing all around as he went. He knew Landon and his terrible friends had broken into the house before in the past, but it could also be Josie trying to get his attention.

As he got closer, he noticed a bright red streak of blood at chest level in the light of the moon. It was smeared across the peeling siding at the corner of the house. A hand, covered in blood, had been dragged across the wall. Lewis could make out the individual finger lines. The smear led to a broken window down the side of the house. An open space remained where boards had once sealed it off.

Lewis turned to run back home—he preferred for the police to come and sort the whole thing out—but then a bloodcurdling scream echoed out from deep within the house. He was sure it was Josie.

Filled with terror, part of Lewis wished Mr. Gray was there to advise him. Ultimately, though, there was only one thing to do. He used the sleeve of his hoodie to push away several pieces of broken glass from the windowsill. He then climbed up into the opening, using every ounce of concentration he could muster to avoid crying out in pain as the ledge pushed horribly into his ribs. He wiggled forward as quickly as he could until he was able to use his body weight to tumble the rest of the way into the house.

It was too dark to see anything as he got back onto his feet. The floorboards were covered in the remains of the busted out window. Shards of glass fell from Lewis's clothing, tinkling as they landed back on the hardwood. The air was musty and stale. No sound broke the silence apart from the crunch of glass beneath his feet as he shuffled them slightly. He hurriedly pulled his phone out of his pocket and illuminated the room with its flashlight. Trash and leaves littered the sides and corners of what was once a dining room.

A scraping sound pulled his attention to the nearby hallway. Lewis didn't want to call out—it felt too dangerous. He took a lunging step to avoid the shattered glass and then moved swiftly into the hallway. The scraping sound continued—it was coming from behind a closed door halfway down the hallway. Lewis hurried to it and silently cracked it open.

Behind the door a set of stairs led down into a basement.

Lewis stepped into the doorway, moving as quietly as he possibly could. A rustling from down the stairs made him think about the passage he'd read in the book about the rogue Parca who'd gone around scaring people into believing in ghosts. Before he could take another step forward, the door slammed behind him into his back. Lewis was propelled down the stairwell, tumbling head over heels. He landed in a pile at the bottom of the stairs, grunting as he tried to regain his breath.

He grabbed his phone from beside him off the floor and then limped, clutching his side, back up the stairs as fast as he could. He grabbed the handle, but it wouldn't turn.

Locked in....

A high-pitched voice called out to him from back down the stairs. "Come back down, Lewis."

Lewis descended the stairs slowly. Mr. Gray was waiting for him at the center of the basement.

"No cell service down here. No one finds you for months," said Mr. Gray. "You die of thirst, alone and pathetic."

Lewis scanned his eyes across the empty basement, hoping to find anything at all that might help him break down the door. The cement slab of the floor stared back at him, mockingly. Apart from Mr. Gray, there was nothing of consequence at all.

"What about my destiny?" asked Lewis. "The decision I'm supposed to make?"

Mr. Gray shook his head. "Don't you see? You already made it when you chose to come into this house. What you do from now on doesn't matter anymore. There are no more decisions that can impact anything."

Lewis felt as if the walls were pressing in on him. "But you can change all that, right? You've got to help me get out of here!"

Mr. Gray chuckled. "No, no," he said. "You have fulfilled your destiny. You were fated to die here from the beginning. You can no longer meddle with immortal affairs. It's for the best."

"The best for who?"

Mr. Gray ignored him. He turned away and walked over to the side of the basement and reached his hands out into the empty air one more time. The light from Lewis's cellphone deadened as it fell across the portal. Mr. Gray stepped forward to leave Lewis to his doom.

"There's one more thing you haven't seen coming," said Lewis.

Mr. Gray paused for a moment and glanced over his shoulder at him.

Lewis dove forward with all his strength, slamming into Mr. Gray like a linebacker. They both tumbled through the narrow opening and into the Beyond.

Beyond

Lewis's head was spinning. Waves of nausea poured over him as his sense of equilibrium spun like a top. He had solid ground beneath his back, but he still felt as if he were falling down an endless hole. His chest hurt—the wind knocked out of him. It felt like an elephant had been sitting on his diaphragm. Trying to focus on the ceiling above didn't help—there was no ceiling, only a shimmering sky that looked like a velvet curtain. There were no stars, only a disorienting swirl of indescribable energy that flowed infinitely overhead.

Mr. Gray stepped up onto Lewis's chest, sending a twinge of pain through his battered ribs. He was smiling down at him. "Well done," said the creature.

"You did it!" exclaimed an even higher pitched voice. A female Parca in a shiny dress that looked reminiscent of a trash bag was standing beside them.

"He looks kind of scrawny. Are you sure he is adequate?" Another male Parca approached on their other side.

"Quite adequate," said Mr. Gray, still staring down at Lewis with a pleased grin on his face. "Do not let his appearance fool you—he is capable of much." He leaned down close to Lewis's face and whispered just for him: "Forgive me for my ruse. The choice to come here had to be yours and yours alone. You've taken your first step towards your true destiny. Welcome to the Beyond!"

Continue reading for a special preview of:

Into the Beyond

Part II : Far From Human

Paul James Keyes

CHAPTER

1

Gray

The starless sky shimmered with the energies of countless universes, shining out from the great Pool of Time like rays of light from the sun in Lewis's own universe. It was a beautiful sight, even within the limited spectrum of vision that a human could perceive. Similar to the infinite depths of the night sky, the multiverse that permeated the immortal realm known as the Beyond was too vast to comprehend. To Lewis, the velvet heavens appeared mostly dark, but to the eyes of the Parcae that stood before him the swirling energies were almost blinding in their glory. The Parcae could see polarization, like the shrimp of Earth, and so kept their eyes cast downward towards the solid mass beneath their feet to avoid becoming disoriented.

The ground they stood upon was not a planet, but rather a rocky plane. Black, obsidian-like stone filled the barren landscape in chunky sheets that crumbled into a webbing of surrounding canyons. Dig deep enough, and one could fall straight out the other side and into the timeless oblivion. Jagged natural formations towered in the distance—steep sided buttes that rose high into the charged atmosphere. It reminded Lewis of Arizona, only blackened… and more alien.

Lewis took the strangeness in without fully processing it. His heart was still pounding in his chest from the jarring transition of traveling between realms. Mere moments before—from his perspective—he was standing in the locked basement of the abandoned creepy house just down the street from his home, being told by Mr. Gray that he was to be left for dead. Then, with all the courage he could muster, he tackled the Parca through his portal and tumbled out of time entirely.

Mr. Gray beamed at him proudly. Lewis's mind was reeling. *He wanted me to go through the portal with him!*

Lewis was one of the Chosen—his destiny uncertain. Chosen by whom or for what purpose was unclear. The majority of people from the mortal realm had preordained paths. They were locked in with the flow of time; puppets reading from a cosmic script. Lewis's destiny, on the other hand, was to be determined by his own actions—of which, choosing to come to the Beyond would prove most consequential. The Parcae could not force him down any path. They could advise and guide him as they saw fit, but it was up to Lewis to choose his fate.

Lewis checked his cell phone. There was no service. He held it up over his head, but it didn't make any difference.

"Did he really just check his phone?" asked the other male Parca. "You're outside of time, boy. You aren't going to find any cell towers out here."

"Don't be mean, Orcus," said the female Parca in a sing-songy voice, "he's still just a child. His brain isn't fully developed yet."

Lewis narrowed his eyes. He tapped into the camera app and took a picture of the Parcae trio. They all screeched and covered their faces from the flash. "My brain is just fine, thank you," he said. He glanced down at the photo. For some reason it hadn't turned out—the whole image was black. He frowned. He wanted photographic evidence that the Beyond actually existed. After deleting the junk picture out of the photo library, he went back into the camera to try to take a better shot, but before he could, the phone turned itself off. The battery was drained.

"Spunky one," said Orcus. "How many tries did it take you to lead him here?" he asked Mr. Gray.

"Many," Mr. Gray responded. "But this isn't the first time we've been here. You two are interrupting my process." He sounded annoyed. He looked back over at Lewis—the boy's incredulous expression demanded answers. "Other versions of you have made this journey before," Mr. Gray explained, "but we've been failing to reach an adequate conclusion. I have a good feeling about this try, though." He gestured at the other two Parcae, "This is Orcus and Adeona—acquaintances."

As interesting as meeting two more Parcae should have been, Lewis was more concerned with the concept of other versions of himself existing. "What do you mean 'we've been failing'? Did I die?"

Mr. Gray frowned. "Not always."

Lewis glanced back up at the swirling sky. It made his head spin with a wave of vertigo. He squeezed his eyes shut, attempting to ground his mind once again. Thoughts of Josie pricked at his heart. He'd heard a scream before entering the creepy house—that's what set everything in motion. "Tell me what happened to Josie," he demanded. "You said the Agares took her?"

Mr. Gray wrung his hands together. "That wasn't exactly the truth," he said. "Josie wasn't taken—she's perfectly fine at your exit point. She plays her part to lead you here quite convincingly."

Lewis was only beginning to realize the true extent to which he'd been deceived and manipulated. "How much did you both lie to me?" he asked.

Mr. Gray sighed. "We told you only what you needed to hear. You don't usually ask this many questions." He glared over at the other Parcae. "You two being here is already causing ripples."

Orcus gestured dismissively.

"Fate has brought us together," said Adeona. "Perhaps this will provide you with a useful set of fresh possibilities."

Mr. Gray considered her words. "Perhaps," he said, "but I have worked much too hard for it all to unravel now. Be gone from here so I may get things back on track."

"May your fates align," said Adeona.

"And yours," said Mr. Gray.

"Shove off," said Orcus. "We were here first. I intend to catch some supper. The path ahead is clear if you must have privacy."

Mr. Gray frowned. "So be it," he said. "Come." He gestured for Lewis to follow him as he wandered farther down the rocky path.

Lewis glanced over at Orcus and Adeona as he walked away. They were already focused on moving rocks out of a divot off to the side of the trail.

"Oow, that's a juicy one," said Adeona as she flung another rock aside. She quickly snatched something up—some sort of juicy grub that squirmed between her fingers. She shoved it fully into her mouth. It made a sick crunch as she munched on it.

Lewis grimaced as he turned back towards Mr. Gray. The doll-sized creature was already well ahead of him down the path. Lewis had to hustle to catch up. Mr. Gray hummed a tune to himself as he stepped gingerly across the loose rocks. Once they finally came to a stop, Lewis began to question him again. "So, Josie was helping you all along?" It was strange to think that Josie's warnings against the Parcae were all lies. He wasn't sure he believed it.

Mr. Gray nodded. "She is quite remarkable."

Lewis began to open his mouth, but Mr. Gray lifted his hand to silence him.

"No more questions," he said. "Everything becomes clear in time." Mr. Gray looked up into the sky, squinting his eyes as he scanned them back and forth. "Just over this way a little farther." He continued walking.

"Where—?" Lewis began to ask.

"—No more questions! I must be precise finding your reentry point." He wasn't the most patient of creatures.

Lewis hated it when Mr. Gray got surly. "I just want to know what's going on," he said.

Mr. Gray continued to gaze searchingly at the swirling energy overhead. "Time in the mortal realm is like a river," he explained. "When you are on Earth, you float down the river at a more or less constant pace. The current of time is too strong to swim against. It all seems very linear to you. The Beyond is like the river bank. Here, it is a simple matter to reenter the mortal realm at any point in time." Mr. Gray's eyes became fixed at a seemingly empty point in space. He abruptly reached a tiny hand into the air and produced a portal as simply as if he'd folded back the flap of a tent. Unlike the dark portals Lewis had seen on Earth whenever Mr. Gray would travel to the Beyond, light poured in through this hazy window. Mr. Gray gestured for Lewis to step through. "Breathe out as you cross—it eases the transition."

Lewis hesitated. Mr. Gray didn't wait for him; he walked straight into the opening, disappearing as he slid between realms. Lewis took a deep breath. When he tackled Mr. Gray through the other portal, he felt like he'd done a belly flop off a high dive. It knocked the wind right out of him. He knew from experience that the portal wouldn't stay open for long. He exhaled hard, emptying his lungs of as much air as possible before stepping forward. He closed his eyes as he crossed through the glowing threshold.

CHAPTER

2

Morning

Lewis felt like he was falling. There was no wind, but his stomach fluttered into his throat. With all the air out of his lungs, he didn't feel like he'd been smacked in the chest as hard this time. The temperature changed abruptly, growing colder as his head spun. Despite the chill, his face felt hot with increased blood pressure pounding at his temples. When he opened his eyes again, he was standing just across the street from his house. The gray light of dawn was beginning to flood over the horizon.

"This is the day we met," said Mr. Gray. "Look." He pointed up at Lewis's bedroom window.

Lewis flinched as the glass suddenly blew out with a bang. In the same moment, the portal he'd arrived through disintegrated behind him.

"That's me appearing. Quick, come hide." He trotted off and ducked behind one of the neighbor's bushes.

Lewis followed him. "Why are we hiding?" he asked. A moment later, Lewis watched as another version of himself leaned out the broken window and shouted into the early morning air.

"Who did that?!"

Lewis and Mr. Gray remained hidden until the other Lewis retreated back away from the opening. After everything that had happened, seeing himself from across the street was officially Lewis's oddest experience yet in life.

Lewis's cat, Melon, was standing in the grass across the way in his yard. He spotted Lewis and came prancing over. "Here, Melon," called Mr. Gray in a raspy whisper. He placed out a pale hand and allowed the cat to sniff him.

Lewis was confused. "I thought you didn't like Melon," he said.

Mr. Gray scratched the cat's chin, instantly producing a low, rumbling purr from the feline. "I didn't back now, but *now* now we have come to an understanding before."

Lewis blinked several times.

Mr. Gray continued, "I traveled back before now and watched you for some time in your past after our first meeting." He gestured up towards the broken window. "I needed to understand you better again after some changes to the timeline. Humans can be so volatile. Melon was very helpful." He stepped up to Melon's side and used the cat's collar as a handhold to pull himself up onto his back. "Follow me," he said. He pressed in with his heels and Melon started walking down the sidewalk with his tail held high in the air.

This must be why Melon was so friendly to Mr. Gray that first day. Later today....

He needed to reorient his sense of time.

Melon trotted down the block with Mr. Gray riding him like a horse. Lewis was barely able to keep up with the unlikely duo. When Melon came to a stop they were standing in front of the creepy house. Mr. Gray dismounted and patted Melon on the head before sending him off, back home by himself.

Mr. Gray proceeded on foot down the side of the creepy house. "I have something for you," he said. "Or more specifically, you leave something for yourself here." Mr. Gray pointed over to where a broken board formed a gap in the rotten fence. "It's in a time pocket." He took in Lewis's confused expression. "To follow the same metaphor as before, time pockets are like eddies in the river of time. They exist within the mortal realm but are outside of time as you know it. Humans cannot see them—not without special tools anyway— but my kind can spot them easily. Go ahead, put your hand in." He gestured towards the broken slat.

Lewis squatted down next to the gap. He felt hesitant. He didn't like the idea of shoving his hand into a random hole— especially one that existed outside of time.

"Don't worry," said Mr. Gray, "there probably aren't any spiders in there."

Lewis paused with his arm stretched out and turned towards Mr. Gray. "Why would you even say that!? Now all I can think about is spiders!"

A boisterous giggle escaped Mr. Gray throat. "I did find a lost badger in a time pocket once."

Lewis couldn't help but crack a smile. "Did you help him find his way home?"

"Oh, no," said Mr. Gray. "Orcus ate him."

Lewis clenched his teeth, his smile fading.

"Hurry, now," said Mr. Gray. "We don't have all year."

Lewis reached towards the fence again. He did his best to ignore the twinge of nervousness that pinched at his insides. As soon as his hand crossed the plane of the barrier his fingers vanished into thin air, completely invisible.

"Deeper," said Mr. Gray.

Lewis groped around as he reached deeper into the time pocket. It wasn't until his arm was all the way in to his elbow that he felt something other than dirt.

"Pull it out."

Lewis grabbed onto the object and pulled it back through the fence. A leather-bound journal appeared as his hand reemerged.

"That contains notes that you thought would have been helpful on your previous attempts at the journey ahead."

Previous attempts...? "How many times—?"

"—Give me your cell phone," interrupted Mr. Gray.

Lewis narrowed his eyes. "It's dead," he said as he took it out of his pocket.

"I know," said Mr. Gray. He snatched it out of his hand. "I'm going to swap it later with the other Lewis's." Mr. Gray started walking away.

So that's why it was dead on the first day of school and already had Kenzie's number in it!

"Where are you going now?" he asked.

Mr. Gray didn't turn around. "I must depart for some time. There is much preparation to be done."

Lewis scratched his head. "Well, what am I supposed to do? I can't exactly go home—I'm already there!"

"Of course not. Don't be silly," said Mr. Gray. "That would be disastrous. You stay here." He pointed at the creepy house. "Read your notes. You explain what must happen." He tugged at an invisible seam in reality and created another portal. He turned back towards Lewis and shot him a little wink before stepping backwards through the opening and leaving Lewis all alone.

Odd little guy. Lewis glanced around, unsure what to do with himself. *I guess I go inside....* He wasn't looking forward to the climb through the broken window again—his ribs were still badly bruised from the beating Landon and Andrew gave him. He walked over to the window anyway and, to his dismay, found it boarded up. He proceeded to search around the entire house looking for another entry point, but every window and door was fully secured. The sun was starting its rise above the horizon. People in the neighborhood would soon be waking up and heading to work. He needed to break into the house before anyone spotted him.

With a broken piece of the dilapidated fence as a pry-bar, Lewis ripped the boards free one at a time from the window until it was left looking just as he remembered it before going to the Beyond. He climbed inside, being much more careful this time not to injure his ribs any worse. His shoes crunched across the broken glass that littered the empty dining room. He made his way to the front of the house, passing the doorway that led to the basement. Gritting his teeth, he eyed the door with a dark glower. He had truly believed he was going to die down there.

Once in the foyer, he sat down on the bottom step of the staircase that led up to the second story.

The journal from the time pocket called to him with its mysterious origins. He held it in his hands, feeling the residual heat of the leather. The pages felt thin as he flipped through them. The journal was tattered and worn out, but the binding still held strong. There was just enough light coming in through the entryway windows to illuminate the words. Turning to the first passage, he recognized the handwriting immediately. It was his own, written in faded pencil:

"Hello, me…" the passage read, "I'll do my best not to sound like Mr. Gray. Hopefully this won't be too confusing. There are some things you must do. I've already done them, and trust me, even though some will sound like the worst ideas ever, I need you to do everything I write down exactly as I describe. It will all turn out for the best. Trust these words over everything else, even over Mr. Gray if it comes down to that."

A note written in a blue pen but still his handwriting was scribbled in the margin and between several lines. "#2 here, I've made some changes. Ignore everything that's been crossed out and follow my new instructions. Things may have worked for #1, but either I didn't follow his (My? Our?) instructions well enough from his description or else external forces have made changes to the timeline that he did not account for. If you screw up, amend this journal and place it back in the time pocket. Good luck!"

The writing changed back to the faded pencil. "Do not read ahead. I've written different entries with tasks that must be completed before reading on to the next. Only read the current entry or else things may get too confusing."

The blue pen scribbled between the lines again. "Good advice. Take it one step at a time. It's tempting to read ahead, but DON'T!"

In pencil: "For simplicity, I will refer to the original me that is living in our house and just met Mr. Gray as Prime." Added in blue pen: "or just P. Short on space sometimes."

Lewis could already tell this wasn't going to be simple. Without actually reading anything, he flipped through the pages again. There was definitely more than just pencil and blue pen written across some of the pages.

How many times has this journal passed through my hands...?

He flipped back to the beginning and continued reading where he'd left off: "Entry 1: Today is Prime's first day of school. You need to go meet Josie at her house one hour before school. ~~Tell her everything and have her read the next page so that she trusts you.~~" In blue: "She knows more than she ever let on. She's on your side. Don't question her. Just tell her today is the day she's been waiting for and get ready for the ride of your life!"

A Note from the Author:

If you enjoyed the novel, I also have another series I'm writing—The Arcadian Complex, featuring my debut novel, Wrought by Fire. The books are a lot longer in that series, as they are aimed at an older audience—a series where I don't hold back on the content. It was and still is a labor of love, and I consider it to be my masterpiece. The first two books are already complete as of this writing, with more to come between Into the Beyond releases. You can read the synopsis of Book 1 on the next page.

Also, please don't forget to leave a **review** online! That, along with telling your friends and family about my books, is the best thing a fan can do to give back. The more attention my novels get, the lower the financial burden of writing them will become (it takes years). I will continue to share my stories, one way or another, because that is what I love to do!

Consider lending this print copy to a friend!

About the Author:

Paul Keyes was born and raised in Washington State between the beautiful waterways of the Puget Sound and the always majestic Cascade Mountains. Fascinated by the political and social workings of the world, he obtained degrees in both creative writing and economics from the University of Washington. In his spare time, he is an experienced pianist and composer, which has helped him bring a heightened sense of rhythm and emotional resonance to his written passages. Over the years, he has traveled everywhere from China to the Mediterranean, soaking in the many diverse cultures and histories. Throughout it all, there is no place he would rather be than back home, drifting on a boat somewhere between the San Juan Islands and his home port of Edmonds.

You can follow Paul on Twitter **@PaulJKeyes**,
TikTok **@PaulJamesKeyes**,
or visit **VergePublishing.org** to become an honorary Chosen!

Also By Paul Keyes:

The Arcadian Complex Series

An Ancient Magic lingers from a Forgotten Era.
Wizards Reign & Terrorize with Godly Powers.

Salvine is sold to a madman who uses her flesh to form a beast with an unquenchable **thirst for blood**. She must do as her masters commands—fetch the head of the bearer of the *Mark of Kings*.

Her target, a man plagued with *haunting visions of a destroyed world*, discovers he can bend both man and nature to his will as long as the moon hangs in the sky. The symbol etched into his bicep is more important than he realizes. He is fated to be king, but only if he can survive a perilous journey across lands ruled by powerful tyrants.

When a local boy named Javic discovers the future king on his farm, he doesn't think his luck can possibly get any worse. If only he knew Salvine—the girl he **secretly loves**—is trapped in the mind of one of their hulking stalkers.

An epic tale of magic and mayhem spans a rich world brimming with danger.

You can find the series on Amazon, or visit the website, **ArcadianComplex.com**

Thank you for reading!
-Paul